TEMPER CA

PAUL SKENAZY

TEMPER CA

MIAMI
UNIVERSITY
PRESS

Copyright © 2019 by Paul Skenazy

Library of Congress Cataloging-in-Publication Data

Names: Skenazy, Paul, author.

Title: Temper CA / by Paul Skenazy.

Description: Oxford, Ohio : Miami University Press, [2018]

Identifiers: LCCN 2018038745 | ISBN 9781881163640

Classification: LCC PS3569.K434 T46 2019 | DDC 813/.54—dc23

LC record available at https://lccn.loc.gov/2018038745

Designed by Quemadura

Printed on acid-free, recycled paper

in the United States of America

"Glass" from *Come, Thief: Poems* by Jane Hirschfield,

copyright 2011 by Jane Hirschfield. Used by

permission of Alfred A. Knopf, an imprint of the

Knopf Doubleday Publishing Group, a division of

Penguin Random House LLC. All rights reserved.

Miami University Press

356 Bachelor Hall

Miami University

Oxford, Ohio 45056

To Farnaz

Transparent as glass,
the face of the child telling her story.
But how else learn the real,
if not by inventing what might lie outside it?

JANE HIRSHFIELD, "Glass"

PART

1

1

It was July—not the skin-scorching July I knew as a child growing up in Temper but the overcast chill of San Francisco summer mornings. I was at my kitchen table feasting on my usual Saturday breakfast of self-loathing, wondering why I needed to drink myself into a hangover every weekend Angie was away. Dad's call was a relief.

"Joy, your grandpa died last night."

"He finally drank himself to death?"

Grandpa Isaac presided over Temper General, the family store, and the mines and houses my ancestors accumulated over the last hundred-fifty years. When I lived near him as a child he smoked cigars and drank bourbon every day. "Never before noon," he liked to say, though only about the cigars.

"Seems that way," Dad said. "I wanted you to know. You used to be close."

"Not that close," I said.

"Don't rewrite the past on my account," Dad replied. I let that go.

"How's Boise these days? The camera store? Madge?" Madge was wife #3.

"Fine, fine and fine. But I'm in Temper. I've been here for the last two weeks."

"Doing what?"

"Visiting old friends," he answered. "The memorial and burial will be next Saturday so the family can get here. Be nice if you came and stayed a few days."

A memorial? Grandpa was a crotchety bastard who made Dad's childhood a horror and put an end to mine. It would be good to see the old man six feet under.

I told Dad I'd be there by Friday afternoon.

"Come to the house," he said.

"What house?"

"Ours."

"Are you camping out?" I asked.

The last time I saw our house in the mid-1990s the windows and sliding doors were gone, the paint chipped and yellow. The roof split under me when I tried to climb to the second story. The surrounding woods were a tangle of broken branches and narrow paths that led nowhere.

"Just come to the house."

2

I was sitting at a stoplight that afternoon when I burst into tears. Once the crying started, it didn't stop. Day after day. I couldn't predict when the bawling would come on: at my desk, cutting radishes and jicama, watching Jon Stewart. Bourbon didn't help.

I thought of calling Mom for sympathy but she was off on her annual month of volunteer work in Yosemite, far from a phone line. Angie was in Houston. She'd become the golden girl of the American Culinary Institute, their financial handywoman who patched up accounting leaks that were costing the company tens of thousands of dollars. Her rescue missions for ACI were lined up like planes waiting for a runway: Houston, Las Vegas, Boston. She'd disappear for three- or four-week immersions in one school after another, then fly home for a week in town with me. I felt pinched into the intermissions of her life like someone stealing a kiss during TV commercials.

The two of us had learned long ago that we ended phone calls feeling farther apart than before we started talking. I called her anyway.

"I don't get it. You hate the man."

"Right. The tears are crazy."

"Do you need me to come home?"

I paused, staring at the calendar. It told me that Angie was off to Las Vegas in less than a week.

"I'm not even sure I'll get out of here on time," she said. "There's talk of a law suit."

I ended up holding Angie's hand, virtually at least. It took her ten more days to sort through the mess. By then I was with Dad in Temper—sleepless, but not from grief.

3

The Sunday after Dad's call I had a gig photographing a wedding. It was after-hours work I did to supplement what I earned writing grants and handling newsletters and publicity for the local food bank. "Temper Photography" my card said. Weddings, bar mitzvahs, christenings, funerals—whatever you paid me for. The extra money let me travel, buy clothes that weren't on sale, and eat out when I wanted.

This one was standard stuff: a large hotel ballroom, tuxedos for the groomsmen, pale green dresses for the bridesmaids. I wandered the room, took portraits of anyone who would stop long enough, and sat at a table with kids playing tic-tac-toe during my breaks. I was packing up my equipment when one of the bridesmaids came over to me, introduced herself as Penny, and asked me for my card. I'd noticed her, and noticed her looking at me. She was tall and thin, small-breasted. She took a great photo: her lean, sharply-featured face with unusually full lips looked even better on my DSLR screen. I found a card, handed it to her.

"Do you have an event coming up I can help with?" I asked.

"I'm not sure," she said. "How about a drink downstairs in the bar, or I call you in a day or two?"

What is it about weddings? This wasn't the first come-on, woman or man. But it was the first time I said yes. Do I thank Grandpa for that, or my ongoing loneliness? I'm still not sure.

The bar led to Penny's hotel room, which led to a game of spin the bottle. I left with my clothes on, hers mostly on, the bed messed, a hickey when Penny turned aggressive, and a date for drinks two days later. The drinks led to her house, an introduction to her roommate Alf, and another evening of almost before a last, long goodnight kiss. We didn't waste time on biographical details. I found out that Penny grew up in Virginia, escaped to college in Austin and worked in IT. I let her know about growing up in Temper, my recent flood of tears, my job, my divorced parents—and Angie. She didn't blink—just gnawed at a new spot on my neck and went to see if she had any more wine in the kitchen.

I knew if I went back to Penny's again I'd stay the night. So I made a date with her for a downtown bar the Thursday before I left to meet Dad. We sat next to each other, our hands on each other's thighs. When we walked to our cars, we held each other for a long time.

"I'll miss you," I said.

"You don't have to. At least not yet."

I smiled.

"Not yet."

She hugged me.

"Text me," she said before she rose on her toes and opened her mouth briefly against mine.

I kissed her back. She reached into her pocket to pull out a miniature silver railroad spike on a chain.

"I saw this. It made me think of what you've told me about Temper."

I let the chain dangle from my hand, then put it around my neck.

"There was no railroad running through Temper," I told her.

"That's OK. It's there now. Or will be once you arrive."

I hugged her, rubbed my hand down the length of her back then up to her neck before I let go.

PART

II

1

I loved to dazzle friends with stories about Temper.

"You really lived in tie-dyes and overalls? Built your own house? Smoked dope all day?" I'd nod and add tales of black bears and wolves—some of them true.

The Temper where I grew up in the 1970s was a far cry from the mining town it once was. My great-great-great-great grandparents, Constance and Solomon, founded the place in 1848 when they opened a general store to cater to the gold-seekers who poured into the Sierra foothills. When the placers gave out most of the miners headed elsewhere. Hardrock mining briefly revived the town, and left the area honeycombed with underground tunnels famous for their ghostly moans. For my fifth birthday Mom and Dad gave me a human skull they claimed came from one of the deserted mines. I called it Solomon, after the family patriarch. I'd rub the top of its head for luck and talk to it every night before bed. I left it behind when I took off with Mom.

I last saw Temper thirteen years ago, at a family reunion Dad forced on me so I could say one last goodbye to Grandma Alice. In 1995 it seemed as tiny as when I grew up there—a backwash bypassed by time. But as I turned east off Highway 49 for the funeral, the AC on full blast in the 98-degree heat, I passed two billboards advertising new housing developments. One offered glimpses of town-house units encircling small pools; the other pictured two and three-bedroom luxury homes alongside a golf course. Where would the water come from for the lawns and fair-ways, I wondered: all I saw around me were the dry, late-summer California grasslands. Moreland Properties offered both developments. Cheryl Moreland, the real estate mogul Dad ran off with. I didn't drive all this way to have to deal with her again.

Temper 2008 was a town, not the jumble of worn road-side buildings I remembered. A small park of young oaks and sycamores had replaced the grocery. There was a stop-light where Main and Vein, the renamed county roads, met.

I drove by a candy and ice cream store, a wine bar, and a bank—a real bank, not the counter and metal grate in a corner of Temper General that passed for a bank in my day. The former gas station was a two-story building, Temper Historical Museum and Jail. The sidewalks were crowded with men and women in shorts and tees carrying packages and holding children's hands. Temper General was a comforting eyesore: the front porch with its wooden steps, the double doors, and the worn exterior in need of paint. It was the only thing that looked like I remembered. I drove through as fast as I could, anxious to find Dad.

In the 1970s, Bitter Root Road was a thin dirt byway: two miles of muddy potholed swamp in the winter and a parched, rock-strewn path in the summer heat. It dead-ended at our house, an A-frame surrounded by a forest of oaks and pines.

When I turned onto Bitter Root that Friday, I found the road had been paved and renamed Ivy Lane. The entry to our house was surrounded by two gated, brick-walled properties that sloped up hills I'd never seen before.

I braked as soon as I turned into our gravel driveway. The house had had a facelift. Redwood steps led up to the deck. Sliding glass doors reflected the late afternoon sun. There was a coat of fresh paint on the outside walls. The roof looked new.

Dad was sitting on the deck, dressed as always—jeans and a t-shirt, wire frame glasses slipping down his nose. He'd lost some hair since last Christmas when Angie and I visited him in Boise. I saw more pride in his smile than he usually let show—or felt, if I knew anything about him.

"Surprise!"

"You did this? When? How?"

"The last five or six years."

"Why?"

"I'd rather you'd have said, 'Wow!'"

"Sorry. Wow. Wow. Wow! Now why?"

One of Dad's shrugs.

"It seemed the right thing to do. And I could finally afford to rebuild."

"Someone die? Besides Grandpa, I mean."

He smiled. "Sort of."

He turned to look at his work, then down at me, still sitting in my car.

"There's watermelon and fresh lemonade inside."

I grabbed my bag and camera. Dad led me through the sliding glass doors into the kitchen: a table I'd never seen before, new Mexican tiles on the counter, new stove and refrigerator.

I was in shock. I sat and picked at the melon and drank a glass of lemonade.

"Want a tour?" Dad asked.

"How about I just wander?"

He nodded.

I walked through rooms that no longer resembled my memories: 2008 upscaled versus 1979 dropped out. The raw plywood floors had been covered with oak. The living room was spotless. A large metal storage cabinet and a folding table stood in one corner. A few enlarged photographs of Grandpa and Grandma were spread across the table. The fireplace sparkled. Dad had ground out the dirt and black stains from the brick hearth. There was a mantle now, with two photos of me: one as a child, one from last summer. Director's chairs sat across from the couch, a small oak veneer coffee table in between. They made a discreet social arrangement in an otherwise vast room that used to be stuffed with oversized pillows and mattresses.

The rest of the house followed suit—open space, new floors, repainted walls, clean windows. There was nothing in Uncle Thomas' old room. Mine had a twin bed with a chair alongside. Upstairs in Mom and Dad's room there was a platform bed, two low night tables and a few clothes hanging neatly in the closet. There was a towel drying over the shower curtain rod, a throw rug on the bathroom floor. The bed was made.

This was not where I grew up.

2

Though Dad left Temper in 1964 the town never left him. It lingered in ways Mom had no hint of until the opportunity to return arrived in the form of two letters: one from Dad's grandfather Amos' lawyer, the other a two sentence note from Dad's father Isaac.

Mom and Dad met in Berkeley and fell in love working for McCarthy in the '68 campaign—Dad still has a McCarthy pin on the denim jacket he wears everywhere. When they graduated in 1970, they got married and went off to Europe to lick their political wounds. Nixon was in the White House, MLK and Bobby Kennedy were dead. Altamont had turned Woodstock into a sentimental memory. Vietnam went on and on.

"We had to get out," Mom said when I asked about those years. "The U.S. wasn't the world we wanted to live in. So we went looking for another one. Little did we know it's the same crap-shoot wherever you go."

The letters found us in the spring of 1974. We were living in Spain, a small town between Barcelona and Valencia. It was one of many European villages we wandered in and out of those first years of my life, almost interchangeable when I try to recapture that time through Dad's photos.

I was supposed to be asleep. Mom was sitting at the table, her hands folded in her lap. Dad was walking back and forth, papers in his hand.

"This is our chance to make a home for ourselves. For Joy," he said.

"We've got a home, David. Here. The three of us. Wherever we are."

"But Temper is where I grew up. It's me, my roots."

"It's not you, not anymore. And certainly not me. You left Temper because you hated it. And your father."

Dad didn't answer her, just continued to walk back and forth, slapping the envelope and letters with one hand while he held them with the other. I lay there quietly, not wanting either of them to notice me.

Mom got up and stood in front of Dad so he had to stop moving. She tried to hug him but he pulled away, stepped around her and went over to the table. I watched him put the letters down, pat them, then bang his fist down on the table. I let out a cry and sat up, so suddenly that they both turned. Mom came over and hugged me.

"It drives me crazy that my father stands in the way of us living off the land the way we've always dreamed we might," Dad said.

"Then don't let him."

Mom said that softly, in a whisper. And with so much love, I've always thought, looking back. Dad must have felt it, that heart offering itself to him.

"Just answer one question," Mom said.

"What?" he asked.

"Are you going back to make a home for us or to spite your father?"

"You know the answer, Harriet."

She did, pretended she didn't, and we moved to Temper.

It was Mom, not Dad, who kept those letters. She showed them to me years later, when I was 13. Mom and I were moving to San Francisco at the time, and Mom was sorting through boxes of photos and papers. Dad's grandfather left him $5,000 and a parcel of prime farmland. Along with the behest came an offer from Dad's father to buy the land from him for $10,000. "The money should support you and that socialist you married until you both grow up and get jobs," he wrote. I've often wondered what Dad would have done if Grandpa just offered the money without the needle. But that was as impossible for Grandpa as it was for Dad not to return to Temper.

When I finished reading the letters I looked up at Mom. At that moment in time—1984—Mom the socialist worked in a yarn shop in Sacramento. Her hair had turned white. She spent her nights knitting afghans in front of the TV.

I asked Mom why she agreed to live in Temper.

"We were young enough, or I was, that I thought we could do anything. Even handle Isaac."

She paused for a moment, staring down at Grandpa's offer.

"We wanted out," she continued. "Any way we could. And there was not much more out than Temper, CA. It was like horse and buggy in a convertible world."

"More rusty pickup if you ask me," I said.

"Your dad wanted to show Isaac he could make a home for himself and us. Something better than the way he grew up."

"How did that turn out?" I asked, knowing the answer.

3

At the end of my tour I stood on the deck outside Dad's bedroom looking out to the trees and creek. Dad came up behind me and leaned in the doorway.

"You approve?"

"It's not something to approve or disapprove of, Dad."

"But it's not what you remember."

"No. No one is where they used to be."

"You don't like it."

"I don't not like it. I don't know it. It's come back from the dead like in a zombie movie."

"It's yours. I've rebuilt it for you."

I stared at him, looked back at the bedroom, then at him again.

"I wasn't there a lot of your life, Joy," Dad said. "That haunts me. I know those years can never be reclaimed. But building is what I'm good at."

"What am I going to do with a house in Temper, Dad?"

"I don't know. Live in it, I hope. Or use it as a way to get out of San Francisco when you need to. Or sell it. I suspect Cheryl would be happy to take it off your hands."

That let me change the subject.

"Why didn't you tell me that Cheryl is in town?"

He was surprised by the question.

"Did you see her?"

"No. Just her billboards. New housing projects? A golf course?"

He nodded.

"And she wants to buy Temper General," he said.

"What does she plan to do with a general store?"

Dad stopped me.

"How about we postpone that topic until dinner. That will give you time to get used to your new home. I opened some wine, put out chips and salsa, and bought a rib eye to grill. You used to like shucking corn."

I smiled, went over, hugged him, and told him how amazing the house looked.

"It's a beautiful gift, Dad. I'm just in shock."

"Good. Stay that way. At least until after dinner."

We ate quietly, both I suspect waiting for the other to start.

I broke first.

"OK. Before we get to Temper General: the money for this remodel? And what are those monstrosities where the woods were?"

"They're the money. About ten years back Madge and I were strapped. So I called Cheryl. I had heard she was doing a lot of real estate in town. I asked her to put most of my land up for sale. She told me I'd get a lot more if I sold it all instead of holding onto the area around the house. But I said no. Even she was astonished with what she managed to get for the rest of the property. Madge and I paid our bills and the rest has gone into this place. Unfortunately you don't have control over what people do once you sell."

I nodded.

"And the store?"

"From what I hear Cheryl wants to convert the store and the warehouse buildings around it into a mini-mall. Dad wouldn't sell. You know Isaac when he's decided something."

"Uncle Aaron and Saul will? You get no say?" I asked.

Dad shook his head.

"I'm not mentioned in the will. No surprise there. I've been trying to talk your uncles into holding onto the store until the dust settles. They won't listen. The recession hasn't been good to either of them. They could use the cash."

Dad started piling dishes in the sink. I pushed him away, told him to sit and found the soap. He was in the living room sorting through his photos when I finished washing and drying.

"I've made copies of all the Temper photos for you," he said. "I thought you might like to have them around once you start using the place."

The world through a viewfinder. Mom and Dad bought a banged-up Airstream for us to live in while they built our house. Once the house was livable, the Airstream turned into Dad's darkroom and Dad's camera turned into his life obsession.

I was looking at some of the photos when Dad glanced at his watch and put his hand on my shoulder.

"I'm glad you're here. Really glad. Keep looking at these. I have to go."

"You needed at the Nugget?" I teased, mentioning the local bar.

"Something like that," he said with a smile. "I'll see you in the morning. The funeral is at nine."

And that was that. Out the door, into his truck.

I went to the kitchen, opened a bottle of beer, then returned to the photos. They brought back the smell of Mom and Dad when they'd take me on their lap at the end of a day with sweat wetting their t-shirts, a beer in hand, Mom with her cigarettes, me with sawdust powdering my hair. They bought me a miniature tool set—hammer, screwdriver, axe and saw—and let me help pull out bent nails and have my way with scraps of board. I would carry sandwiches out for the crew and munch my way through the day on potato chips and Kool-Aid. Late afternoons I'd escape the heat by standing in the creek or wandering off into the woods.

In the few photographs Dad let someone take of him he wears shirts torn at the neck, a Paul McCartney beard, John Lennon glasses and grins awkwardly at the camera. What I didn't notice when I was younger is how much he looks like his father. I stared at the blowups Dad had made of Grandpa Isaac for the funeral service. The resemblance was unmistakable. Dad did his best to disguise it with his beard, glasses and long hair. But the shape of his face: that was Isaac. The eyes weren't quite the same: Isaac's were round and recessed, Dad's narrower, almost pointed ovals. But the nose, the slightly protruding ears, and the forehead and receding hairline were a match. I wondered if Mom recognized the similarities those years we lived here, and if she ever mentioned them to Dad.

My Polaroids: where were they? I think it was my sixth birthday when Mom and Dad bought me the camera. All their friends chipped in for what seemed an unlimited supply of film. I would snap pictures for a while and then forget about it. I'd find it again and shoot everything I could, night and day. Then I'd misplace it. Eventually I lost it somewhere, or left it behind when Mom and I left town.

I hadn't thought about those shots for years. I couldn't imagine Dad getting rid of them; he was a pack rat when it came to photos.

I felt disoriented—Dad, the house, Grandpa, Temper. I took an Ambien and texted Angie.

Surprises. Could use you and your bookkeeping skills.

Houston was two hours ahead, so I didn't expect an answer that night. Then I sent another text, to Penny.

You're on my mind.

She wrote back immediately.

Let me know when I get to your lips.

4

Temper, Saturday morning. A perfect day for a funeral.

It was already hot when the sun woke me at 6 a.m. I heard Dad upstairs. A bag of coffee and a French press were waiting on the counter. While the water boiled, a beep told me I had a text. It was from Angie.

Crazy here. Might get to SF next Wednesday if you're there.

I texted back.

Depends on Dad.

Angie must have been near her phone.

Let me know. If not I'm going to Vegas. A hint about the surprises?

I'm house rich. And Cheryl's around.

OMG!!! Can't wait to hear.

Dad was awkwardly adjusting his tie when he came into the kitchen.

"I didn't know you owned a suit, Dad."

"This is your Uncle Saul's. I asked him to bring an extra for me."

"The tie and shoes?"

"His too. Shoes are a little tight but otherwise a good fit, right?"

"You'll do," I told him, giving him a hug before I went off to dress.

As we drove through Main Street I saw that all the stores were closed, with signs saying they'd open again at noon. Black ribbons draped one entrance after another; the flag in the park was set at half-mast.

Dad saw my surprise.

"It's always been this way for the Tempers, though I've never been sure if the town closes down from respect or fear. Doesn't matter, I suppose. This is likely the last time."

"Last of the Mohicans," I said.

"What?" Dad asked.

"Grandpa said that to me once, about himself. We were walking in the cemetery. I didn't get what he meant. 'The end of the line,' he told me."

"Sounds like him," Dad said. "Managed to forget me and my brothers, and you."

He didn't forget. I decided not to tell Dad the rest of what Grandpa said. "Aaron and Saul ain't coming back here except to put me in the ground," he told me. "Your dad—I don't know where he came from. And you're a girl. Not your fault."

I changed the subject.

"I couldn't find my Polaroids last night. Do you remember where they went?"

Dad didn't say anything for a moment.

"You gave those to your grandfather."

That rang a vague bell.

"Why would I do that?"

"Your mom and I wondered the same thing."

"What'd he do with them? Any idea?"

"No," he said. "I can't say."

5

When we arrived in Temper, Dad's high school friends awaited us: Amy and Bobby, Gwen and Charlie, and Preacher, who moved through too many women to keep track of. Josiah Baldwin II was his full name but we already called him Preacher because of his dad, minister of the local Congregational church we went to each Christmas Eve. I remember nights around an outdoor fire when I would fall asleep with my head in Mom's lap while the adults imagined their utopias. Next morning I'd wake up huddled between my parents, encircled by three or four couples sleeping on mattresses strewn across raw plywood.

Dad liked to say he was a redneck by day, a hippie by night, a student in his dreams. Mom hadn't so much as nailed picture hooks to the wall, but she learned fast. They designed as they went. You could do that in Temper then— no one to inspect, or no one you didn't know. Work halted for days from lack of funds, then would leap forward in more flush times. Downstairs consisted of a kitchen and living room along one side and two bedrooms on the other. Steep stairs led to a narrow hallway, bedroom, and bathroom. We had a small garden where Mom grew broccoli, beets, lettuce, tomatoes, and corn.

And cannabis. Dope was our cash cow. We didn't bother with details—CBD, THC, and ACDC were all the same to us. Life was simpler then: plant, nurture, harvest, sell. In plastic bags or Saran Wrap. At the Nugget, our local tavern; at Tony's Diner; in the grocery aisles; at our front gate. Even behind Temper General if we were sure Grandpa wasn't around. Everyone knew, no one said.

Mom's brother Thomas arrived the summer after we settled in town. He'd just come out of the Navy. Mom told me that Uncle Thomas used to be a good amateur boxer. Those days were long gone, though he still looked muscular. But he was slow, vague. Soft in the head, Mom said. He had a way of holding my hand that I cherished—not squeezing, not asking for anything, just holding. He called me "Miss Why" because I asked so many questions.

The day we met he walked up to me and formally introduced himself:

"Hello. I am Thomas. Your uncle. I am coming to live with you."

I giggled, then curtsied, as I was learning to do in kindergarten.

"I'm Joy Constance Temper. Your niece."

Then I hugged him and we were friends.

Uncle Thomas moved across our lives erratically, like a listing ship in need of a port for repairs. He'd leave, return, and leave again. No one except Mom and me took much notice. When I asked him where he went, his answers confused me:

"I get this idea there's something I need to find."

"What?"

"Not something like a thing. Just something. So I go look for it."

"And you come back after you find it?"

He smiled.

"No finding. Just looking. When I get tired of looking, I come home."

When Uncle Thomas was at home he'd go off for hours in the afternoon, tromping around the hills.

"Still looking?"

"Under every rock."

6

The church was nearly full, family on one side of the aisle, townspeople on the other. Dad sat with his brothers and their wives in the front two pews, the rest of us spread behind. Cousins I barely knew whispered to each other while their kids played with devices in their laps, earbuds hooked into iPods. Everyone was sweating. The surprise was to see Cheryl Moreland standing at the back of the church. She nodded her head when she saw me staring.

It was hard not to stare. Cheryl was dressed in dark denim jeans and a checkered shirt. She was tall and thin-waisted, with breasts that stood out as straight and pointed as if she were a teen. Or had them fixed, I thought to myself, as I turned around and saw Preacher rise to begin the ceremony.

I hadn't seen Preacher in years. He looked like he belonged here in church, the robes accenting his height. His deep voice carried down the aisles and commanded attention. He started the service by recounting the generations of Tempers who had left their mark on the town.

Uncle Aaron and Uncle Saul spoke briefly about Grandma and Grandpa's dedication to the store. Dad's homage was a row of photographs that lined the altar. Preacher got up again at the end.

"Isaac loved this town. He was skeptical of outsiders. He did not suffer fools gladly, and he thought most people who disagreed with him were fools. But he was not unkind, at least not always, and not to everyone."

Did I catch Preacher glancing at Dad? Dad turning his head down for an instant to avoid the glance?

"Not unkind, just impatient," Preacher went on. "He didn't have time to waste. He said to me more than once, 'Preacher, I'm a dinosaur. I've lived too long. My world's gone.' But he refused to sell out. He never wavered."

Preacher let the silence settle and turned to the closing prayers.

———————

A backhoe waited alongside the grave. It was a smaller crowd now, the family in their suits and ties, a few older men in jeans and checkered shirts. The coffin was lowered into the ground and people took turns covering it with handfuls of dirt. Some stopped to mumble something into the grave. Dad didn't take a turn and neither did I. At the end, Preacher picked up the shovel, put a pint bottle of bourbon on top, and laid it on the coffin. "For the journey ahead, Isaac," he said, and all the old men laughed.

Then we stood quietly while the cement slab was lowered into place atop the coffin. I glanced sideways and noticed a woman standing alone about thirty yards away. She was dressed in white: blouse, shawl, hat, gloves. It was hard to make out her features. I remembered seeing her in the church as well, sitting near the back on the family side. I elbowed Dad:

"Do you know who that is?"

"No idea. I noticed her myself."

Just as he spoke she turned and walked away.

7

We drove to the Pine Cone Inn, a new resort in town, for the reception. I hated it immediately: its false log cabin exterior, the pine cones that lined the parking lot, the Indian blankets that covered the lobby walls. Three stories high, it extended around one edge of the lake, with a series of separate cabins that branched off in both directions.

The company felt no more accommodating than the Inn. My aunts and uncles were polite and insistent that I say hello to one relative after another.

"Jacob, Adam, Ben, Matthew, this is Joy, Uncle David's daughter. The one who left Temper with her mom and lives in San Francisco."

It was a code. Dad's name, mine, Mom, the city: the hippy kid, turned into a lesbo. Her Dad couldn't keep a job; his wife left him when he started fooling around with that rich bimbo. Only Temper girl born in generations. Can you imagine what her mother's genes must be? A Warning to Us All.

I wondered for a moment if I were imagining the twitches in the cheek muscles and the sneers from the children, congregated in gossipy little groups around the food tables. Then one of the boys—one of Uncle Aaron's grandchildren, if I remembered the introductions right—came up to me after a few nudges from his cousins.

"Where's your camera?"

I smiled but didn't get it.

We stood that way for maybe five seconds more before he said, "I heard you hired out for funerals," then turned and rushed back to his friends.

I headed out to the balcony to look at the water but found it no more inviting.

"They call it Duck Lake now," someone said at my side.

I turned and found the woman in white next to me, a cup of lemonade in her hand.

I studied her for a moment. Asian, I thought, but wasn't sure. She had a pale face surrounded by straight black hair that ended just below her long neck. Her face looked old, but not. There were wrinkles along her ears and across her chin but none on her pale cheeks. She stood straight, without any of the stoop-shouldered appearance of all the elders in my family except Grandma Alice.

"It was called Pompoc in my day and doubtless had another name when the Maidu lived here," she said. "But no one knows what that might have been."

The lake I remembered was longer, misshapen, with a dozen inlets Dad would row in and out of some Sundays. As I got older I could reach up and grab leaves from the trees that shadowed the shores. It had that awkward asymmetry that only earthquakes, winter storms, and Sierra snowmelt could devise. Duck Lake on the other hand was perfectly circular.

"Are you from here?" I asked.

"I used to be. I grew up in a cabin along the far shore."

Chinatown, I remembered suddenly, though by the time I lived here it was just muddy walkways, cracked foundations and broken timber.

"Did you know my grandfather? I mean Isaac?"

"Yes. But I haven't seen him for years."

"It's nice of you to come to his burial."

She smiled.

"I was curious how he'd be remembered."

"And?"

She stopped for a moment to stare across the water, as if at her old home, then turned to me.

"Isaac is not someone you forget easily, however long it's been."

"He's not someone I remember fondly," I said to her. "But no, he's not someone I can forget."

She smiled, put down her drink, opened a small white clutch, pulled out a card and pen, and scribbled a phone number on the back. Then she handed it to me.

"Come see me and we can talk more about Isaac, just the two of us," she said.

LUCY JIN

HEAD LIBRARIAN

SONORA BRANCH

TUOLUMNE COUNTY LIBRARY

SONORA, CALIFORNIA

I looked up from the card and saw she had already closed her clutch and was walking away.

"When should I come?"

"When you need to, dear. I'm officially retired but I run the place just as I used to. I'm there every day. Even Sundays, though then you must call ahead so I can let you in."

She gave me a brief hug. I watched as she moved quickly through the crowd, not stopping to speak to anyone.

8

The first time I met Grandpa was the September after we hit town. We avoided Temper and Temper General that summer—drove the extra miles to buy our food and building supplies in Jackson or Sonora. He surprised us in the middle of the afternoon. Dad was working on the foundation with Preacher while Mom cleaned up the remains of lunch. Grandpa drove up in a battered Ford I got to know well over the next years. He stood by the truck, scoured the scene, then sniffed like he smelled something rotten. Dad stood up, wiped his hands and walked partway over to his father.

"Isaac," he said.

Grandpa looked at Dad as if he'd never met him.

"Where you getting the wood from?" he asked.

"Sonora. Jim Beecher," Dad said.

"Not grade A. But don't matter none to me. Just know your money ain't good in my store and never will be."

He started to open his truck door as if he were done but stopped for one last poke.

"Good you have these boys to help you. Never could saw a straight line to save your soul."

Dad smiled.

"What do you know about carpentry? You're a store clerk. Always have been."

Mom came up to Dad and put her hand on his shoulder. He shrugged her off, turned his back on his father and pretended he was talking to Preacher, who stood nearby, quiet as the sun was hot. Grandpa waited a moment, then got back into his truck and drove away.

9

That night I asked Dad why he didn't like his father.

His face got red, like it tends to do even now when he's ashamed.

"I try not to bad-mouth people," he started. "I guess it comes down to the fact that I didn't do anything right. Or what he called right. When something I did or said wasn't what he wanted, he'd hit me on the back with his belt— sometimes with the buckle, and I'd have welts for days. Might be because I spilled milk onto the table at breakfast. Or because he didn't like the way my boots looked after I polished them. Or because I tore a button off a shirt or got some spot on it that wouldn't come out. It didn't matter how old I was. The worst was when I was slow doing figures in the store. 'No Temper dumb as you, boy!' he'd say. He'd grab the ledger book and smack me."

Dad stopped to stare at Mom.

"He was worse to your Grandma Alice, though I don't want to go into that."

He paused.

"Your uncles say he never hit them. And I think he stopped hitting Mom too after they were born."

Dad kissed me on the forehead and said good night. I heard Mom and Dad talking for a good while. I didn't think anything about that night until two weeks later. Mom cleaned up early from working on the house, cleaned me up, and put a dress on me instead of the overalls I lived in. Then we got in Dad's truck and drove to town.

"We're going to meet your grandma and grandpa," she said to me as we drove.

I sat up straighter.

"Does Daddy know?" I asked.

She kept looking at the road but nodded.

"Your grandma wants to get to know you; she drove up and told us so. And I told your father that maybe your grandpa would look on you a little more kindly than him."

"Did Daddy think so too?" I asked.

She smiled.

———

"All he said was, 'Can't be worse.'"

We parked in front of Temper General. Grandpa was sitting on the porch with some other men. They all got quiet when Mom marched me up the front steps.

"Isaac," Mom said. "I don't care what happened between you and David or if the two of you ever talk again. But this is Joy. She's your grandchild. She needs grandparents. And you and Alice are the only ones nearby."

The men got up and disappeared down the steps. Grandpa stared at us, not moving. Then Grandma appeared in the doorway, wiping her hands on an apron. Mom looked up at her and smiled. She looked prettier than the pictures Dad had, and taller. She held herself so upright, like her back was against a wall. She came over and took my hand.

"You like ginger snaps, bubble gum, or jujubes?" she asked me.

I nodded, not sure what the right answer was.

"A bit slow," Grandpa said, looking at Mom. "Doubt that's from our side of the family," and spit.

Grandma gave him a look and walked me in to Temper General. I don't remember what I ate, but I tasted most every candy they sold over the next four years.

10

I'd had my fill of the reception, my family, and Duck Lake. I went looking for the bar.

Two mock saloon doors in the lobby led to the Bear's Lair. Blood-red leather cushions covered the backs of chairs and booths. There was a large mirror behind the bar, doubling the array of liquor bottles.

I was nursing a beer when I felt someone's hand on my shoulder and caught a heavy whiff of perfume.

"Joy Temper! As I live and breathe!"

Cheryl.

I smiled, took her hand off my shoulder, and stood so she wasn't staring down at me.

"I'm so glad to run into you, Joy. You haven't changed a bit!" she exclaimed. That made no sense; I was twelve when she'd last seen me. I'd grown nearly six inches, not to mention breasts and hips that were still boyishly small twenty-five years ago.

Cheryl on the other hand seemed to defy time. Her face was lined across the forehead and cheeks with patches of pigment where the sun had done its work. But that just made her more attractive. She had cut down on the cosmetics. Her lips were thin, the crimson lipstick of my childhood replaced by a soft pastel that made her mouth recede into her face rather than announce itself as it used to.

"Dad told me you were in Temper," was all I could get out.

She nodded. "I run this Inn for a group of investors. And I'm working on several real estate deals."

I looked down at my beer for a moment, then picked it up to move away. She put out a hand to stop me.

"Look. I know you don't like me. But I want to talk to you. Twenty minutes. Please."

I stared at her, put the beer down and slid into my seat. Cheryl moved around the table to the lake side.

"Thank you."

She looked back to the bar and lifted up her hand. A waiter came over. Cheryl ordered a martini. I asked for bourbon, neat.

"You'll no doubt hear about the town meeting the day your grandfather died. Isaac and I really went at each other. I . . ."

"What about?"

" 'The soul of Temper,' to use his phrase. He still published that rag of his, you know? The *Temper Times*?"

I remembered it from childhood, when I would help Grandpa by carrying copies to the stores downtown the first and sixteenth of each month. He listed me on the masthead as the "Distribution and Sales Manager" though the papers were free and most of the ad space was for his store. When Grandpa saw that I could hold a camera steady, he would sometimes hand me his Instamatic and tell me to bring back a photo of Tony in the town diner or of one of his friends sitting on the front porch of the store. Or a pony that had just been born. Sometimes he'd use my photos, sometimes not. When he did I'd get a tiny credit.

"I don't want Temper's soul," Cheryl continued.

"Just Temper General."

A pause while the waiter set down our drinks.

Cheryl smiled.

"I wanted to make Isaac rich."

"I never pictured you as Mother Teresa," I said.

She sipped her drink, chewed an olive.

"I didn't expect it would be easy getting Isaac to sell. But he'd been drinking so much he hired high school kids to manage things."

I didn't say anything.

"Did you know Isaac planned to start mining?"

"The China Mine?" I guessed. "He was talking about opening that when I was a kid."

"I think he meant it this time. He hired geologists to determine if it was feasible. There is still gold underground. With new techniques, the price of gold what it is, some people think it's worth trying—especially with the recession. I don't want that around here. The new mines near Nevada City destroyed the streams."

"This is a mining town."

"Was. Now it's a place for people to imagine their way back to that time."

"Sell the illusion," I said.

"Isaac was still living in the 1850s, wanting to turn back the clock."

"So do you, but just as pretend."

"I've heard that before. Isaac couldn't win. He must have known that. I have too many rich, patient backers."

"You wait out the opposition."

"Exactly. Just like your family did a century and a half ago when they accumulated land offering next to nothing to penniless, disappointed miners."

I started to protest, but Cheryl didn't give me time.

"Do you know how this town started?" she asked.

"When Solomon and Constance came here and opened the store."

She smiled with what seemed vindictive pleasure.

"Yes and no. There was a little settlement before that. El Arroyo Pacífico. A few Mexican families lived here and worked on a nearby ranch owned by a Spaniard named Martinez. Solomon got himself land from the U.S., came in and took over."

"How did he do that?"

"Same way all the Americans did. They swarmed in after gold and ignored the claims of the Californios and the native tribes. When the U.S. won the 1848 war, the treaty said they would honor the traditional land grants. But that never happened. There weren't a lot of courts around, and those that were favored the Anglos, like Solomon, over Spaniards or Mexicans. Poof. Temper and the rest of California were ready for statehood."

"It's got to be a little more complicated than that, Cheryl."

"Sure. But walk into that little museum downtown sometime and look around. It might open your eyes about your family. Check out the exhibit on the Chinese who lived here while you're at it—hundreds of them, mining, feeding the miners, washing their clothes. Paying taxes to Solomon for the right to mine. Foreign miner's tax, it was called. Twenty dollars a month. Solomon got himself appointed magistrate."

She seemed happy to see me upset.

"Is this the way you defend your own greed?" I asked.

"None of the Gold Country towns tell the real story of those years. About the Californios, the Chinese, the Mexicans who came north from the mining districts around Sonora, the Chileans. It's time someone brought all that out, instead of mocking the whole thing with tourist shops that sell coolie hats and panning sets, and hiring people to per-form Mexican folk songs."

"Cheryl the home-wrecker has turned into Howard Zinn."

"Who's that?" she asked.

I'd finished my drink and my patience. I stood up.

"I think I'll head back upstairs," I said.

Cheryl stood too, alarmed.

"Just a few minutes. I'm sorry I got off on your family's past; you just unnerved me."

She smiled.

"Like you did when you lived with David and me."

I stood there, waiting for her next move.

"I'm not sure you'll ever talk to me again but there are a few things you need to know. About what went on."

Her neediness fed my animosity—and my curiosity. I sat down again. She did, too.

"I'll be quick. I suppose it doesn't matter to you but I really loved your dad."

"So did Mom," I snapped back.

"I didn't destroy your life. I might even have saved it."

"You fucked with me when I was a kid, Cheryl—with me and my parents. I don't give a damn what you wanted then, or what you want now. You must know that."

"You don't know anything about me. Or your parents. Or yourself. Or what really broke up your little Eden. I tried my best to make a home for you."

I smirked.

"I wasn't altruistic. I wanted your dad, and you were part of the package. But it was also a chance to be the mother I didn't think you'd had and figured I'd never have another shot at."

I was trying to find my wallet; I didn't want Cheryl paying for my drinks. She kept talking.

"Your mom and dad failed you. Don't you know that yet? Not just them: all those creatures who spent their time in your living room getting high and fucking around. You were a ragamuffin. They let you run wild, forgot to feed you. They didn't even clean your underwear."

I turned back to her, wallet in hand.

"Where do you get this shit?"

"Your father told me."

"I don't believe you."

Cheryl shook her head.

"I know you took your mom's side. But I tried. I bought you what you wanted, taught you how to sit, walk, talk, look like a girl, act like a woman. Your mother never did that and never would have."

She paused while I fumbled with my wallet.

"You've got more of me in you than you want to admit. Your mother didn't teach you to wear a black shift like that, or accent it with knee-length boots, did she? And is that the pearl necklace I made your father buy you?"

I couldn't wait anymore. I dropped a twenty-dollar bill on the table and turned toward the lobby doorway. Cheryl threw a parting shot at my back.

"Ask your folks about the spiked Kool-Aid and why your grandfather wanted to take you away from them."

I started back towards Cheryl, ready to choke her. I noticed two half-filled glasses amid the used plates on a nearby table, grabbed them and threw the contents at her. The water landed across her face, the top half of her Western shirt, and her lap. She started swearing, struggled to stand. I turned and headed out the swinging saloon doors.

11

Grandma Alice came from a wealthy banking family down in Sonora. When she married Grandpa, they opened a branch of the Sonora Bank in a corner of the store. It had a metal grate for a window, a stool, a cash drawer, and a waist-high safe Grandma's father contributed. It was open 1–3 Monday, Wednesday and Friday. "Convenient," everyone said. People could do their banking and get their supplies at the same time. When the bank closed for the day Grandpa would check the ledger against the cash to make sure every penny was accounted for. By the time I was five I was helping him, either sounding out the account names and numbers or counting the cash. He'd test me: make me multiply and divide in my head, add and subtract three and four figure amounts. He'd grunt when I got them wrong or didn't work fast enough, nod when I solved the problem to his satisfaction.

"Money ain't something to fool with," Grandpa liked to say. "You don't make friends by being poor." Grandma always found a way to slip a nickel or dime into my hand or pocket every visit. Grandpa contributed in larger amounts, less frequently. If I caught some irregularity that passed him by, he'd pull out a quarter, and once or twice handed me a silver dollar.

"You've got the knack," Grandpa told me one day.

Mom liked the fact that I felt at home with my grandparents.

"It's nice for Isaac that you are so good with things. Your father can be a bumbler. It's part of his charm, if you ask me. I never have understood how he took to carpentry and his camera so easily."

"Maybe because Grandpa wasn't teaching him," I said.

I associate a particular odor with that time, of cigars and Four Roses. Grandpa would start drinking anytime. "Sipping the day away," he liked to say. If the store was empty he would sometimes shut early or leave Grandma in charge and take me fishing. He was prouder of his casting skills than he deserved to be, but that was probably true of most of his prides. If the fish weren't biting we'd get in his car and head out into the hills. He'd point out properties he owned as we drove, tell me the story of how little he paid for this place, how he bargained for that one. If there was no one living in one of the houses, we'd stop and he'd let me run around through the empty rooms or make up stories of the family who might live there while he stood outside or sat on the front steps smoking a cigar. The big excitement of those days was heading up to China, the abandoned mine he owned. It was in the hills a few miles from town, with a clearing nearby. The entrance was a wide, rectangular upside-down U created by two posts and a heavy crossbeam. Despite two knee braces, the top beam curved downward, warped by years of pressure. You could still see bits of wood left from the structure that once must have covered the surrounding rocks.

Grandpa would take my hand and we'd walk the trails for a time, or make a small fire in a nearby clearing in winter. He'd bring a flashlight and we'd search out the mine itself for a hundred feet or so. He would ask about school, listen to me ramble on, sip his whiskey. He liked to comb my hair; he said Dad and Mom never bothered to get out the knots. He didn't say much beyond that about Mom and Dad. It was as if they were creatures from another universe who slipped off their spaceship and landed in Temper. Different DNA, different hearts and souls. I seemed the only alien creature exempt from his contempt.

"You're a natural. A Temper through and through."

12

Those summers in Temper were like letting an animal—me—out of a cage. I didn't know I'd been in one, but the woodlands unlocked me. I lived running from one tree or sound to the next, distracted by a hoot or crackle from a bird or the noise of squirrels rushing along a downed log. I entertained myself with garter snakes and howled into the dark at what I thought were wolves in the woods behind our house. I invented mushroom demons. Fallen branches became dinosaurs and elephants. I hid in the cold mossy clumps of autumn leaves. Sometimes I slept in a lean-to I called my cabin. An old rattler skin was a talisman I used to talk to black bears and owls that haunted my nights. I remember bringing home used condoms, cracked mugs, rusty beer cans. A rhinestone ring I found that was big for my fingers wound up on a string around my neck for months.

My grandest claim to fame: from when I was five I knew how to hold scorpions so they couldn't sting me—hold them the way I now do carrots or celery, eggplant or some rosemary I want to hang upside down to dry. This was as fundamental a part of me as being a girl. I'd track the creatures as they made their way along the shadows of gravestones or rocks at home, and then appear with one thrashing between two fingers, snarling a little while I calmly held onto it. Dad still insists that "scorpion" was the first word I could write, long before my name, though I've never believed him.

Grandpa gave me my nickname one day when I arrived at his store with two scorpions, one dangling from each hand: "Well, if it ain't my little Scorpion Queen!" The other men sitting on the front porch laughed. I rushed up to one after another; they jumped away from me with a whoop.

I want to believe I remember the touch of them: the slight resistance as I'd grab one at the edge of a pile of wood scraps or stones. Even now I can imagine their wooliness. I liked to stack them, one atop another to see how many I could arrange before one moved enough to upset the balance. Mom told me not to torture them but she'd smile when I'd bring one over to show her with the pride of a cat depositing a dead mouse at the door.

I know I went to school when I was supposed to—I still have my report cards to prove it. But mostly I remember days in the trees and nights at home surrounded by Mom, Dad, and their friends. The people seemed almost interchangeable: Amy making bread or soup in the kitchen, Charlie lighting a fire or yelling that we were out of paper towels and could he use the work rags for napkins, Gwen tucking me in.

Uncle Thomas was my favorite. When I told him about spending time with Grandpa at the China Mine, he looked at me hard for a moment, then asked:

"Your grandpa tell you about the ghosts?"

I swung my head back and forth. From then on he'd offer tale after tale about the men crushed by rock slides who spent eternity watching over other mournful and hapless miners. It was as if he knew them personally. When I asked if he did, he put his finger to his lips, turned his head in every direction as if making sure there was no one around to overhear, gave a small nod and said,

"They don't want a lot of people to know. But you're OK—they told me."

I promised to keep their secret.

13

I wanted out of the Pine Cone Inn but realized I was without a car. When I went to find Dad, I saw the reception was still going strong. Dad and Uncle Aaron were talking to a pot-bellied man in a sheriff's uniform.

As I approached the group, Uncle Aaron lifted his voice, looking angrily at the man.

"Jesus, Norman. What do you think you're up to? He died of old age and booze. There's nothing to investigate."

The Sheriff was quiet, then mumbled an answer I couldn't hear.

"Unusual circumstances my ass. Stop meddling."

Uncle Aaron stomped off. The Sheriff stood watching him for a minute, turned and saw me. Dad introduced us.

"This is Sheriff Norman Gray. We went to high school together."

The Sheriff lifted his cap and bowed slightly.

"Sorry about that," he said. "And sorry for your loss."

He nodded to Dad and headed towards the door.

I looked at Dad, who was following the Sheriff's back as he walked away.

"Norman told us that when he examined your grandpa's body at the mortuary he found scratches all over his arms. He wants to know why."

"He could have gotten scratches anywhere in the woods, Dad. Especially Grandpa, the way he drank."

Dad nodded, but didn't answer.

"Uncle Aaron doesn't think it's worth worrying about?" I asked.

Dad nodded again.

"Anything else I should know?"

He looked surprised by my question.

"No," he said, shaking his head. "Not yet, anyway."

Dad has this elusiveness I've gotten used to over the years. He'll hold back a story he isn't ready to let out. What he says when he finally decides to talk makes me wonder why he's so closemouthed. It's a tic that has always made me feel like he doesn't trust me to understand. Or to love him if I did.

I started to ask something else but Dad kissed my forehead.

"Preacher was looking for you. He asked if you'd come by and see him."

I nodded. Old home week.

"Where have you been, by the way?" Dad asked me.

"Talking to Cheryl. She corralled me in the bar.

"I've had enough of all this," I went on, swinging my arm to indicate the room. "Can I take your truck? You can get a ride from someone?"

He smiled, reached into his pocket for the keys, then looked away.

"I won't be home until morning."

I nodded, started to turn away.

"I'm missing something," I said. "Where are you sleeping?"

"I've got a bed. See you by noon."

At the house I changed clothes and nibbled on leftovers. The heat was relentless and by seven p.m. I was sweating sitting in a chair. I ran up to Dad's room, grabbed a towel, got my swimsuit and drove to the quarry, the local swimming hole. I stripped off my shorts, stuck my feet in the water to cool myself, and then dove in. I swam to the opposite bank and back again, sat watching the shadows lengthen and cover the surrounding hills, dressed and headed back to my car. Then I drove to the China Mine, took my flashlight from the glove compartment, and hiked up to the entrance. The last time I saw it, almost thirty years ago, it was boarded up; now it was open again. I flashed light at the ceiling, where bats hovered. A few whisked by me.

As I wandered up a nearby path, I stumbled over something and flashed my light on it.

It was a spatula. The edges were rusted, bits of dried food clung to the top. A few ants were crawling over it. I dropped it and circled the flashlight over the nearby bushes. A bit of metal glinted. A military dog tag in that familiar racetrack shape was stuck between two branches. It was shiny, no rust on it anywhere. Also no embossing, de-bossing, or key chain. I'd seen these online selling for a dollar a dozen. I stuck it in my pocket.

Beyond the bushes was the clearing I remembered; in the center of it the ashes of a campfire. I thought I heard movement in the bushes but it stopped when I waved the flashlight in that direction.

I went back to the mine. About twenty feet in I saw something stuck in a crevice in the rocks. I pulled at it. It was a brown wool blanket. Behind that was a duffel bag.

The bag was worn, the zipper rusted. It kept catching when I tried to open it. Inside I found a pot, a fry pan, a metal plate and coffee cup, a fork and spoon, a pair of torn jeans, two tired t-shirts and two briefs. I zipped the bag back up, put it and the blanket back where I found them, and headed home.

14

The sun woke me early again the next morning. The house was quiet. No Dad. There was a text from Angie.

How are you? Where are you?

Good. Sad. Glad to be with Dad but he's not here. He rebuilt the house, you can't imagine.

You're right, I can't. I've never seen it. You've never invited me, remember? Take photos. Give him a hug for me. Love you both. Gotta go.

After my first cup of coffee I walked through the house, taking photographs of each room. I walked outside and circled the house, shooting as I went. Then I walked down to the creek. There was a new picnic table there like the one on the deck, sawdust still surrounding two of the legs. I walked along the banks in both directions until my neighbors' walls stopped me, slid down into the water so I could peek briefly around both. I didn't like what I saw, and headed back to the house. Antsy in this no longer familiar home I'd just inherited, I set off to town.

The walk was quiet except for dogs barking, pulling at chains or sticking their noses through fences. The houses were small, set back behind dry lawns. There were no sidewalks. People parked on their front lawns or along unpaved driveways. I saw small plastic children's wading pools, gnomes and flamingos gracing small gardens of rocks and moss, a wall of beer cans cemented together with a cat asleep on top. Few cars passed in either direction. A heavy balding man was sitting on a chair, hose in one hand, slowly swinging the nozzle over his garden. He noticed me, smiled:

"Going to church?"

I was dressed in a t-shirt and shorts. I shook my head no.

He nodded, turned his face up to the cloudless sky.

"Nice morning for the Lord."

I nodded back, smiled and moved on.

Town insulted me. I knew I was being a snob but that didn't change my mind. Stores offered household goods, local weaving, pottery and jewelry. Cheryl's idea for a mini-mall would fit in just fine, I thought, J. Crew butting up against a toy store specializing in Yosemite Sam and Stinky Pete dolls. I went to the market, bought eggs and pasta, and headed back the way I'd come.

My phone dinged. A text from Penny.

Miss you.

I stopped walking to write back.

Miss you too.

The reply came immediately.

What are you up to?

Walking. Sweating. Getting barked at by dogs.

Then a long pause while I slowly hiked back home. I was near the house when Penny wrote again.

How are the drinks at the Pine Cone Inn?

Good in the bar. Why?

I'm deciding what to order.

WTF?

Come over. Bring your swimsuit.

Where are you? Really.

Poolside. In the shade. I burn. Stop texting. Come.

Penny. In Temper.

I ran the rest of the way. Dad still wasn't home. I stood at the side of my bed for a long minute staring out the window at the weeds and trees. I was about to do something impulsive so I pretended I could think it through. All I did was repeat the rationalizations I'd been giving myself for months—Angie absent and inattentive, Angie apologetic but choosing work over me, Angie and I waltzing around each other but never into each other's arms. Or almost never. I flashed on our mornings when habit trumped feeling and we circled each other with the harmony and precision of clock hands. I grabbed my towel and swimsuit and headed to my car.

Penny was waiting underneath an umbrella that covered two lounge chairs. A pitcher of margaritas and two thick glasses with salt on the rims sat on a small table between the lounges. Her swimsuit was a mismatched bikini, red top and yellow bottom.

I walked up, bent to her face, and gave her a brief kiss. She reached to the table and handed me a plastic room card.

"Room 205. Corner. Or I think there's a restroom down here to change in."

"Come up with me."

"Now?"

"Why wait?"

She laughed, got into her flip-flops and poured drinks into the glasses. We carried them upstairs. I pushed her onto the bed. The triangles of her bikini top went first. She gave me little time to kiss her breasts before she was pulling off my tank top, then tilting me over, alongside her, so she could slither out of her bottoms, I my shorts. She held me down while she bit into my neck, then moved her tongue slowly over my body, inch by inch until I pushed her head between my legs. I came, quickly, a tremor that convulsed me. I tried to pull her up for a kiss but she resisted, grabbed my hand, kept her mouth, tongue and hands

---

moving. I felt another spasm, then another—slower, prolonged—that started with a scream and ended with me murmuring long guttural sounds as I gradually came back to the bed, the room and the woman who now lay atop me.

We didn't stay that way long before I flipped us over, found my way down her body and felt her hips pushing against my face. Then she was at my neck, her teeth biting into the soft skin just below an ear. I flinched, cried out, and started to push her away. But she held tight, went to my lips, and bit down on the bottom one until I tasted blood. I screamed again, but she quickly licked the blood off with her tongue while her hand reached inside me. The pain vanished. And so it went until, exhausted, we stretched out quietly and reached for our drinks. It took us another hour to find our way to a shower and the lounge chairs by the pool. The pitcher was gone. We ordered another and passed the afternoon that way, barely speaking. Not saying anything worth remembering anyway, in and out of the pool. Then upstairs to her room and bed again.

———————

It was near morning before I thought to ask her.

"Why me?"

"Why me?" she asked back.

"You first."

"I want what I want. I don't ask questions. I stopped that shit years ago. I wanted to kiss your freckles from the moment I saw you at the wedding. I now know that they're not only all over your face and neck but on your legs too. I loved our two nights together last week."

"So you got in your car and came here."

"Exactly."

"Were you that sure of me?"

"I told you, I don't think things out. We met, we clicked, and we made out. Your hands felt good. I wanted to see what that was all about."

"It sounds so simple."

"Isn't it?"

I paused, unsure of myself.

"And what's with the biting?"

She laughed.

"Lust is lust. There's no half-ways for me, girl. Be prepared."

I took that in, let it ride.

"How long can you stay?"

"I'll call in sick tomorrow. And maybe Tuesday if you want."

"I want."

"Tell me again Tuesday."

I rolled over, kissed her, and promised I would without saying a word.

15

When I turned into our driveway at 10 a.m. on Monday, Dad was sitting at the edge of the stairs writing on his yellow pad of paper. It turned out he was home the night before.

"To have some time with you, hon."

He brought some trout with him for dinner.

"Did you eat it?" I asked, avoiding all the questions we weren't asking.

"Nope. Hungry?"

I wasn't after a big meal at the hotel.

"Starving! Haven't had a trout breakfast since I lived here."

"I'll start it. There's a pot of coffee waiting. You might want to wash your face."

He got up, left his pad on the steps, and went into the house. When I looked in the mirror I saw blotches of lipstick at the edges of my mouth. I wiped them off as directed, then headed into the kitchen for my third cup of coffee.

———

The trout was already in the cast iron pan. Butter was bubbling up. In another pan Dad had potatoes and onions sizzling on one side and bacon crisping in the other. He gave me a quick glance, then turned back to the stove.

We took our coffee with us to picnic table by the creek. He handed me a key.

"This is for you. I've got one. And there's a spare duct-taped underneath this table."

"Like it used to be when we lived here."

"I learned that trick from Dad. Not much else, but this has been useful."

I was quiet, watching the creek. Dad surprised me, starting things immediately.

"I hear she's pretty."

"Hear from who?"

"From Amy. She saw you at the pool. She was there with her grandkids."

No secrets in Temper.

"Does she have a name?" Dad asked.

"Penny."

"Penny. Is she nice?"

"I don't know. Yes. To me."

He smiled.

"I just met her a week ago, Dad. She didn't tell me she was coming to Temper, just texted yesterday from the Pine Cone Inn."

"It's nice, the Inn."

"I think it's awful."

"It brings in business. They do a lot of local hiring."

"I guess that's good. It's sure luxurious."

Dad paused to sip his coffee.

"Angie doesn't know?"

I shook my head, tried a countermove.

"You see a lot of Amy when you're here?"

"I try to see all of my friends. Gwen and Danny have moved off. Bobby's still here, and Preacher. I have a beer at the Nugget, go to the quarry for a swim."

"And see Amy."

"Yes."

"Alone?"

"I'm not sure I want to talk about that with you."

"Is that where you go nights? To her house?"

He was quiet.

"What do you remember about how we lived when you were growing up?" he asked.

I told Dad about falling asleep to the noise from the grownups and how when he and Mom weren't around Amy or Preacher or Gwen would make me sandwiches and tuck me into bed.

"Your mom's never talked to you about any of it?"

I didn't know what he was getting at.

"The way we all lived with each other?" he asked. "How we put what we earned into a common pot? Worked and ate together?"

I stared at him.

"I'm not sure what you're asking me," I told him. "I mean I guess I knew that. Sometimes I think I only remember what you took pictures of. Since I talked to Cheryl I'm starting to wonder if I've made up my whole childhood."

"What did she say?"

"She confused me is all. She said I was a ragamuffin. How you and Mom and the others were all . . . uncivilized."

"Hmmm. I wouldn't say that. But let me think a little. I'll get back to you."

I started to ask something, realized Dad was not going to tell me more, and got angry. I hate feeling stupid.

"That's all I'm going to get? 'Let me think a little'?"

"For now."

I got up and turned to the stream. Like the lake at the Inn, the water had a new name: "Prospector Creek." That didn't seem to bother the fish; why did it bother me so much?

I went on the attack.

"Is Amy the reason you come back?"

"Enough. Really," Dad said.

He put a finger to his lips. I stopped, waited, and impatiently focused on his hand. I could see the row of calluses along the top of his palm. I heard the whirr of a neighbor's generator, the sound of the creek, the wind shaking the pine needles. I made a turn.

"It's great what you've done with the house," I said to him, "but I don't understand why you bother coming back here. It's not Temper anymore."

He shrugged.

"It's Temper. It's just not what you want it to be."

"That's OK with you?"

"I don't get an OK. Do you?"

I didn't have an answer.

"Temper's not the same." Dad said. "I'm not the same. I can't control that."

Then one of those pauses of his while he glanced up to the empty blue sky—those pauses that make me wonder if he is smarter than he lets on or dumber than I want to believe.

"Or maybe we both are more the same than we think."

I left that alone.

"I went out to Grandpa's mine," I said to him. "The night before last, after the funeral. When you were off with I-can't-ask-about-it."

He gave me a look.

"Someone's camping there, or near there."

He perked up.

"How do you know?" he asked.

I paused for a moment, trying to register his tone. I stuck my hand in my shorts pocket, rubbed my thumb over the blank dog tag.

"There was a duffel bag hidden in the mine, with men's clothes and some pots and pans in it. And a brown wool blanket."

He listened, nodded, looked away from me to the stream.

"Anything else?" he asked.

"A rusty spatula. And this."

I pulled out the dog tag, handed it to him.

He took it and turned it over in his hands like he'd never seen one before. Then he handed it back. He tried to be nonchalant.

"Have you told anyone?" he asked.

I shook my head.

"Why don't we keep this to ourselves."

I started to protest but he stopped me.

"You're going to ask why, and if you do I'll tell you I can't explain but need you to trust me. And you'll get angry and feel stupid the way you do when I won't open up. And we'll be right where we are now. So let's skip all that this once."

I opened my mouth, saw his face and stopped myself. I nodded.

"You'll tell me soon?"

"When I can. I promise," he said.

"OK," I said. "For now."

"That includes your mother," he said, sternly.

"What's she got to do with this?" I asked, annoyed despite myself.

He didn't answer, turned the conversation away from the duffel and blanket.

"You can't find those moaning caves everywhere," Dad said. "You remember Solomon, the skull you used to talk to?"

"You knew about that?"

"Sure. It was how we found out what was on your mind."

I hadn't imagined anyone listening and wasn't sure I liked the idea. I hadn't planned to ask him about what Cheryl told me but it burst out.

"Will you talk to me about the spiked Kool-Aid and my dirty underwear?"

He looked at me like I had spun him by the shoulder.

"You remember that?"

I shook my head.

"Cheryl told me. She taunted me, actually. I threw a couple glasses of water on her when she did."

Dad laughed.

"Do you miss her? Cheryl?"

He thought a second.

"I guess not. She wasn't as awful as you thought though. She taught you a lot."

"That's what she said. How to sit at a table and eat food with a knife and fork. How to dress."

Dad nodded.

"That seems right. Your mom and I didn't think much about stuff like that. We never owned matching silverware. Secondhand china suited us fine. And we never worried about clean or dirty."

I thought about Mom's wardrobe, still a collection of old jeans and used blouses, t-shirts and baggy sweaters. I loved the way she looked but they were Mom, not me. Or not me anymore. Cheryl was right when she called me out on my mourning outfit: it was her all over. I like nothing better than tight jeans, bright-red and orange tops and a stylish wool coat to ward off the San Francisco chill. My jewelry spreads across our washroom countertop, hangs from hooks, too often finds its way onto the floor, where Angie might stumble over it. My clothes fill eighty percent of our closet, prompting periodic protests from Angie about my excesses. "You could dress a whole homeless shelter with what you don't wear," she's admonished me, more than once.

Still I found it hard to think of myself as a Cheryl clone.

"Cheryl didn't think your mom and I took good enough care of you."

"She said something like that."

"Did she?"

"She said you were worried about me."

He didn't answer for a moment.

"I was. Maybe worried isn't right. I felt there was something off with how we lived."

"I always had what I needed."

"You made it easy on us. But I think we took advantage of that and too often let you take care of yourself."

"It doesn't seem to have done much damage."

"I hope not."

"And at night? When everyone was in the living room drinking or eating? The communal thing? I was around then too, right?"

"What is it you want to know?" Dad asked me.

"I don't know."

I stopped and waited. It took him a while.

"You weren't at the parties too often. We'd wake you with our noise sometimes, and you'd come in, rubbing your eyes and looking for us. You'd spot your mom or me, or Amy or Tommy would come over and take you back to your room. One of us would sit with you until you fell back to sleep."

He paused for a moment.

"Sometimes I think we were a little too high to know what to do with you."

He sat there staring at his hands.

"Tell me about the Kool-Aid," I prompted. "I remember drinking Kool-Aid. A lot of it. All day most days. Mom and Amy kept making batches of it in the kitchen. I do remember that."

"That was when we were working. That and beer kept us going when it was hot."

"Did you spike it?"

He smiled.

"No. Mostly we just drank it. We sometimes put gin or vodka in during the day. Not often. We didn't want to saw off fingers. There were a few nights we tried acid. We couldn't get it all the time. It wasn't like the movies. We couldn't afford it. But when we could we'd have some at night. In orange juice."

"And you gave me some to drink."

The million-dollar question.

"I don't know."

I stood up.

"Dad! Please."

"I really don't. I know you did drink it once or twice because of the way you reacted. I know I never gave you anything spiked to drink. I know your mom didn't and Tommy didn't. Preacher and Amy and the rest: I can't imagine them being that stupid. But you got it somehow. There were a few nights, one really bad one, when you disappeared into the woods."

Dad was staring down at the table, rubbing one hand across it.

It came to me like a jigsaw puzzle, the edges done, a few center pieces that fit together, and a lot of random ones that I couldn't place yet. It was dark. I had no idea where I was going or why. I didn't have any clothes on. I stumbled over something—a root or plant limb. I saw myself leaning against a tree trunk in the dark, my eyes squeezed tight. The world I knew was gone.

I told Dad what I was seeing.

"I'm not making this up?" I asked.

He shook his head no.

"I looked for you all night," he said. "It was morning before I found you. I wrapped you in my jacket, picked you up and talked to you. When I asked you to look at me you screamed and started to bang your fists on me so I told you to shut your eyes again. You bit me and yelled at me to let you down but I just held you tighter while I walked back to the house. Somewhere along the way I felt you relax. By the time we got home you were asleep. We put lotion on all your scratches, and kept a warm towel on your forehead. You slept until the next night."

I didn't say anything, watching the scene play out as he spoke.

"Was that the only time?"

"There were other times when you ran off, but not far and not for long. We'd see you take off or Tommy or Preacher would alert us. That time was the worst."

I nodded.

"I think that's enough for now," Dad said.

I nodded again. He got up, pulled me up and gave me a hug.

"I'm sorry that happened. Part of why I ran to Cheryl is that I knew you'd be out of danger. I hoped she'd clean up the mess I'd made of things."

Then he turned away.

"I need to go."

He kissed my forehead, and started walking away.

After a few steps he turned back, looking more at the oak tree than me.

"I don't know if you'll understand, if you're old enough. After a while, you find out—or I think I've found out—that it's not who you sleep with or who you don't or how often that means much. It's also what happens years later—years after you do the stupid things you wish you'd never done. It's how you find your way back, the way you and me have, more or less, to what we are today.

"What I'm trying to say is that what matters, long view, comes down to who you spend your time with. Who you sleep with night after night. Like beside, next to. The one who lets you pull the covers off at night and still makes you coffee in the morning. That kind of love."

I stayed quiet. Dad wasn't one to talk about himself like this.

"I didn't know that with your mom. Back then I couldn't imagine the stretch of years I've lived. I've had time to make amends with you. I didn't give myself that chance with your mom. I didn't know that kind of pleasure could be enough, more than enough. Now I'm older."

"And you know what you want."

"I just know my own way. And I'm lucky. You are here and seem OK. We love each other and love to camp and take photos together. Madge and I get along. Right now I'm really lucky."

I watched him walk slowly back to the house hitting himself lightly on the leg with a branch he picked up on the way. It was another fifteen minutes before I realized I hadn't asked him what any of this had to do with Cheryl's parting shot about Grandpa.

16

Penny was waiting for me at the Inn. She showed me two matching sleeveless t-shirts she'd bought in the lobby souvenir shop that said "Prospectin'" across the breasts in rhinestone glitter. I tried to explain that my family never prospected.

"That doesn't matter. We're prospecting now, right?"

"For what?"

"I have no idea. For what we find. Each other."

She insisted I try the new tee. It made me feel like I had less on than in my spaghetti straps. I changed back to my own top.

"I know you came for the funeral," Penny went on. "But now that you're here, there's something stuck in your throat, right?" she asked.

"What?" I challenged.

"I can't tell you. I don't think you know. But you seemed to be afraid of coming back here."

"Did I say that?"

"Not in so many words. But you did say you weren't just crying about your grandpa. And you didn't suddenly run into my arms because of my nail polish."

I didn't want to hear anymore. I pulled her "Prospectin'" tee over her head, kissed her, and moved us to the bed. We spent the rest of the afternoon at two wineries that had sprung up in the hills outside town. Then it was back to the Inn, the pool, the Jacuzzi and her bed—a nap this time, side by side, holding hands.

At night I drove Penny to the quarry. It was empty. She insisted we strip down and swim naked.

"I want to see your ass in the moonlight," she said, dropping her own shorts and turning her bare butt to me. We swam out, back, out again. We lazed in the shallows, reaching for each other under the water. When we got back to the Inn we lit the gas fireplace and watched Katherine Hepburn on TV. Penny had the ability to wash away worry.

But I woke more than once that night. I *was* afraid to come to Temper alone. I deserted Angie for deserting me. Now I wasn't alone. And no less afraid.

I wondered if Dad ever felt like this.

17

I knew Penny had to leave Wednesday afternoon and thought I was ready for it. But the day went wrong from the start. As we headed across the lobby after breakfast a woman behind the front desk called her over.

"A Mr. Temper left a package in your name. He said it was for a Ms. Temper."

It was an old-fashioned hatbox of bright red felt with decorative branches and leaves festooned across the top. Penny wanted to open it immediately but something told me to wait until we got back the room.

Inside was a skull. The eyes were recessed and there was a hole where the nose belonged. Cracks ran down the cheeks. The forehead was smooth, though, and there was a significant frontal bone. The man—I guessed a man from the size—must once have been long in the chin. A Post-It was attached: "Been saving this for you. Time I returned it. Dad."

Solomon. I started to cry, looking across the wide bed at Penny. She stared back, then came over and held me while I went limp in her arms.

"Is this your dad's idea of a joke?"

I couldn't talk yet, so I nodded yes, then no, then yes and no again.

"Not sure" was all I could get out.

We stood that way for a minute or two, Penny holding me while I stared at the skull resting on the unmade bed. When I let go Penny went over and picked it up.

"Heavy!" she said, cupping it in her hands for a moment. Then she tossed it into the air.

I pulled it away from her the instant she caught it.

"Don't!" I yelled. She stared at me, shrugged, and began to pack.

18

I wanted Penny to see the cemetery.

"Macabre," Penny said. "But it's your dime."

When I lived here the cemetery was my kindergarten. I'd go there with Dad. He'd stop in front of Great-Grandpa Amos's stone, clean up the dead leaves and bring along a cloth to wipe dirt from the marble. He'd prop up a fence that had toppled or straighten a family gravestone. I'd try to sound out names—Abraham, Grace, Eustace, Jacob. I learned numbers by reading the birth and death dates, and could eventually recite the inscriptions. I'd bring along crayons to make maps of the gravesites and try to copy the sayings.

I needed to reattach myself to something, and the gravestones were what I trusted most. I longed for the quiet, a place where I'd find no altered street names, round lakes or false storefronts.

***

We drove in separate cars. As we walked through the family plots Penny reached for my hand, kissed the palm, then pulled it tight to her breast. I tried to disengage but she held on, her other arm around my waist. I told her about the first time I visited the cemetery with Grandpa when he came to put flowers on his grandmother's grave.

"When I asked him if he brought the flowers because he missed her, all he said was, 'You're supposed to.' He said it was a way to let the ghosts know you're watching. 'They don't surprise you that way.' That was him all over."

"I can't stand flowers," Penny said. "They die before you turn your back on them. It's like giving death to the dead."

The Temper family graves date back to 1854, when Solomon's wife Constance died. Through 1890 the family spreads out more or less symmetrically, with angels marking the women, lambs for the three children lost to the fever in the late 1870s, and a shovel and pick shaping an "X" across the top of the men's, however little prospecting they did. The rest of the graves are more haphazard. Some just have birth and death dates, some brief sayings, some angels or lambs decorating the stones. Aunts and uncles, great-great-great-great and I suppose not-so-great-grandparents and a mess of cousins—they're all buried here, waiting for me.

Penny and I walked slowly from grave to grave, bending down to read the faded script on the old stones. But Penny would reach for me, move her hand along my arm to my shoulder and down, then to my waist. She tried to pull me close for a kiss but only made us stumble as our feet got crossed. When I bent to clean some dirt from a canary-like bird on one stone, Penny grabbed me from behind, pulling me back against her. The two of us would have toppled to the ground if I hadn't held onto the stone for balance. I straightened and moved away, not saying anything. Penny drifted off too, and started reading the inscriptions aloud. "Blessed in Memory." "A Mother Above All." "He Never Left Us Alone." The words started meaning something they weren't supposed to. Then she made up more. "He Kept His Own Counsel." "Attentive to a Fault." "Honor Was Her Lost Virtue." "Bigger Than Suspected."

It wasn't anything, I tried to tell myself. She didn't know these people. She knew I didn't know most of them either. I was there to connect with the past. She was there to play. I tried to ignore her—take in the dry grass, the wilted flowers and the stones scattered haphazardly over the hill. This little patch of light and shadow, all these people, my kin.

Penny walked towards me, a smile on her lips, her arms wide as if herding me. She got me in a bear hug, pulled me down onto Great-Uncle Jonah's bench, sat on my lap and kissed me. She started undoing my belt.

"You ever screwed in a graveyard? I haven't."

She just didn't care—didn't care whose relatives these were, how they'd died or what they had to do with me. And she didn't get that I cared or notice that I wasn't laughing.

I turned my head this way and that, trying to avoid her lips even as I felt that breathless eagerness for Penny that had become so familiar the last two days.

When she went for my neck with her teeth I pulled my head away.

"Stop," I said. "Please. Penny. Stop."

She didn't answer, put her teeth over my ear—half a nuzzle, half a bite. I squeezed my arms between us and pushed. She lost her balance and fell to the ground.

I stood up.

"You can't do this. We can't. Not here. Please. Where do you think you are?"

I was panting, unsteady on my legs.

"In a graveyard, Joy. Alone with the corpses. Come on, girl. One last fuck in honor of the Tempers."

She wasn't smiling when she grabbed one of my arms, still out in front of me like a guardrail. I tried to call her name but my voice disappeared as she swung me around in an arc and let go. My momentum carried me against a tree, where my head banged the bark before I steadied myself.

"Are you crazy?" I yelled, my head still echoing from the encounter with the trunk. "I didn't bring you here to fuck."

I started to say more but Penny was on me, angrier than before. She put her hand over my mouth and pushed her body up against me until my back was pinned to the trunk.

"Why not here? Are you worried what the relatives might think?" She lifted her hands from my mouth and bit into my lower lip. I swung my head side to side until I felt her loosen her hold. I pushed against her chest, creating a small space between us. She had my other arm pinned back, my body stretched around the trunk.

She went for my mouth again but I kept turning my head to one side then the other, my free hand banging at her shoulder, her chest, then her chin. My swings didn't faze her. She freed the arm she held, deflected my blows and slapped me across the face. She reached her hands to the side of my face to steady it while I continued beating my free hand against her shoulder. She probably could have done what she wanted then. But she let go, pushed off me, and backed away. I slid slowly to the ground and went into a ball, pulling my knees into my chest.

"Forget it, Joy. Go back to your ghosts."

She turned and walked down the slope to the side of the church. I sat there, folded into myself. I could have been there a minute or five, I don't know.

Penny was sitting in her car. Her eyes were closed, as if taking a nap. I stood at the window a moment before she looked at me.

"You hurt me," I told her.

"I didn't mean to. Not at first, anyway. But I can't stand righteousness."

"It's a cemetery. My family is buried here."

"You're not. At least not yet. Not when you're with me. I thought you quit playing by the rules."

"Not all of them."

"If you want to play with me you play. Just play. The no-rules rules."

I think I was supposed to smile. I didn't. I stared, wondering who she was.

"I know you're living with someone," she said. "I'm fine with that. I thought we might have something and I don't give a rat's ass how we find out. We do have something. I'm not just a convenience, you know that. What I don't get is why you think this backwoods shithole is worth a second thought, relatives or no relatives."

She started the engine, made the 'phone me' gesture with her left hand, began to pull out, and then stopped.

"I'm not one for advice. But dump the skull and beat it out of here fast as you can before they bury you with the rest of your clan."

Then she drove off.

I hurt—lip, arms, back and neck. A part of me already missed Penny. The rest wanted to stick a knife through her. I didn't have the strength to do either. It took all the energy I had to walk to my car, close the door, start the engine and back up. If anyone had been behind me I would have run them over.

19

I needed a hug. I went to find Dad, the best Temper had to offer along those lines. When his truck wasn't in the driveway, I thought he might be at Grandpa's house, sorting through Isaac's keepsakes with his brothers. But no. I parked anyway, got out and went up the two steps to the door. It wasn't locked so I walked in, thinking I might wash my face and find some bourbon; I couldn't imagine Grandpa would ever let himself run out.

The house reeked of tobacco; the floors were dark with stains. A day bed sat along one wall. The bed Grandma and Grandpa used to sleep in was gone from their bedroom, replaced by a battered and scratched classroom desk under one window and stacks of the *Temper Times*—yellowing, criss-crossed piles of 11 × 14 sheets of newsprint that came up to my waist. They leaned precariously against one wall of the room.

I looked for the earliest date. Jan. 24, 1948. The hundredth anniversary of Sutter's Creek, I realized. Of course. If Grandpa produced one issue every other week that added up to . . . almost 1500 editions. Most of them were three or four pages stapled together, a few a little longer. What possessed Grandpa to publish all these years, month after month? And to preserve a copy of every issue?

I decided those answers could wait until I found the bourbon: three partially empty bottles in a cupboard in the kitchen. Combined they made a comforting quart. I cleaned a glass, walked back to the bedroom, and then went looking for the *Temper Times* issues from the 1970s when I lived here. I found most of them—all of them, in fact, except 1977, 1978, and 1979. After forty minutes of reading about cows, tractors, used cars for sale, a town meeting to talk about telephone service and weekly weather reports, I was bored. I lay down on the floor, dog-tired, and glanced over to the beaten-up desk. The underside of the desk had mounds of tape stuck to the bottom. There were eight or nine lumps with nothing but duct tape visible. I thought of the house key under the picnic table. Grandpa and his systems.

I pulled at a lump of tape. It came off quickly in my hand, the adhesion mostly gone. I found myself holding a small stack of Polaroids. The prints stuck to each other. These were the photos Dad said I gave to Grandpa. No. The memory came rushing back: Grandpa stole them.

I tore off all the tape, accumulating a pile of photos beside me on the floor. I found a paper bag in the kitchen, dumped the photos in there and brought the bag out to my car. Then I went back in search of those absent years of newspapers. I moved to the living room, let my eyes circle the furniture, and then flattened myself on the floor next to the day bed. More tape. The cheap newsprint crumbled in my hands. I took what scraps I could, carried them carefully to the car, went back for the bourbon and drove to the house.

20

Dad still wasn't home.

I parked, then assembled my hatbox and skull, the bourbon, my Polaroids and the newsprint on the table alongside Dad's photos. I stared at the empty space in the skull where the eyes once were. Did Solomon really steal the land from the Spanish settlers? Of course he did, I realized, the same way the Mexicans and Spaniards stole the land from the Maidu.

I took off Penny's necklace, and slipped the dog tag onto the chain. Then I put chain, tag, and rail spike on the table. I went to the kitchen for a glass, poured myself a double, and went back to the photos. Where to start: Polaroids or newspapers, newspapers or Polaroids? I felt like one of those fairy tale princes with a choice of doors. Behind one were asps, hungry alligators or ferocious tigers. But maybe, just maybe, one hid the beautiful princess.

I chose Door Number 3. I downed the whiskey, picked up the bottle and walked to the creek.

The harsh morning light woke me. I was lying in bed. I had a rank taste in my mouth and an awful headache. The first thing I saw was vomit on the sheets and pillow. I heard Dad moving around upstairs. He must have heard me as I stood—carefully—and inched my way to the bathroom, then kitchen, keeping one hand on a wall for balance.

"Bad night at the office?" Dad asked, once he was standing next to me.

I barely nodded. He helped me sit down, offered me three Tylenols, and poured me coffee and water, both of which he made me drink before he would let me do or say anything. Not that I wanted to or could.

"You put me to bed?" I asked him.

"Uh huh," he said with a nod. "I got home around five. I saw your car and went to the creek to look for you. You were lying face down across the tabletop."

I nodded. That made my head ache.

"I'm packing," he said after I had downed the water and

coffee. "Madge called this morning. She's sick and the store needs tending. I was just supposed to be here a week or two this trip. Now I've been away almost a month. Will you come upstairs when you can?"

I nodded again, sat quietly for a few minutes, and poured myself another cup of coffee. I carried it and myself slowly up the stairs.

His suitcase was on the bed. I nestled onto the floor of his closet the way I used to when I was younger.

Dad reached around me for clothes, glanced my way going into and out of the bathroom grabbing his shaver, tooth- and hairbrush. When he closed his suitcase, he pulled a pillow off the bed, came over and sat down a few feet from me.

"Want to tell me what's up?"

I went through the last two days with Penny—most of it anyway. I held off for the moment on the Polaroids. Dad listened quietly. The coffee was cold but I sipped it between sentences. When I stopped talking he sat and looked at my face for a long minute or two, then glanced up at the empty hangers above our heads.

"What Penny did to you was awful. No one deserves to be treated like that. But I think she's right about your ancestors. The dead don't care if you're interested in them or not. That's for tourists, that Gold Rush, first settlers malarkey. And the cemetery: Preacher will tell you it's sacred ground. It's only sacred if you think it is. I do, mostly, like you. But maybe it's OK if other people don't."

Dad stopped.

"Anything else you want to tell me?"

I shook my head and put my hand on his knee.

"Thanks," I said, both of us understanding that I wasn't only referring to the way he took care of me last night.

He nodded.

"What's going on about Grandpa?" I asked.

"The Sheriff is launching a full investigation. Aaron erupted, though I'm not sure if it's because he doesn't want ugly details dragged up or because he thinks that will delay dispersal of the estate.

"I only know a few details. Dad's fingernails had dirt in them, and not the sort he'd get at Temper General. However drunk Dad might have been, the Sheriff is sure the scrapes up and down both arms couldn't have come from a tangle with branches when he was fishing. Norman says Dad's chest looks like a boulder landed on him. He asked me when was the last time Dad was up at one of his mines. I said I didn't know."

"Did you tell the Sheriff about the duffel bag?"

"No. But you should when you have a chance."

"Sure," I said. "As soon as I sober up, deal with Penny, figure out what to say to Angie and try to explain all this to Mom when she calls—which should be today or tomorrow. What did I forget?"

"The photos and newspapers in the living room."

I nodded and made a mental note not to underestimate Dad as much as I did.

"How about we look at them together?"

He helped me stand and hobble down the stairs.

21

Dad had carefully pried the Polaroid prints apart to retain the image. I turned them over one by one. Some of them Dad must have taken, since I was in them. But most were mine. My very first photos. They should decorate a wall, I thought, like the first dollar bill you see in some diners. A lot of them didn't belong on a wall. Underneath the desk—yes; that was an ideal burial ground.

I lowered my head onto the table and started to cry. Dad sat next to me with a hand on my knee. When I was done, I got up, washed my face, came back and looked at Dad.

"You knew about these," I said.

"Yes and no," Dad said. "I knew Isaac discovered them thirty years ago. I didn't know Isaac kept them."

"You didn't want to tell me about them."

"It seemed like you didn't remember much. I thought it might be better if you kept it that way."

"Like not remembering the night in the woods? The acid? The dirty underwear? Who did you really think it would be better for?"

"I was thinking of you, Joy. I've never believed that truth sets you free."

"Lies don't, Dad. Or maybe you've decided they do?"

"I can't imagine how these photos can make you feel better."

"I just got assaulted trying to make myself feel better."

Dad didn't say anything.

"They're my way back in time," I said. "You're the one who taught me that. They help me remember what I saw, who I was, who you and your friends were. They bring back Uncle Thomas."

"What else?"

"What do you mean?"

"What else do they help you remember?"

That stopped me.

"Tell me."

"No. When you remember you tell me."

"What are you afraid I'll find out?"

"What they did."

With that Dad stood up, pulled me up and gave me a hug. He went to get his bags.

I walked him to his truck, still angry.

"You're really going to leave me like that?" I asked him. "In the dark about the photos? Grandpa? The duffel at the mine?"

"The dark's not so bad. It's the best place for developing."

He looked back at the house.

"I've got a few things left to do here but it's pretty much what I once dreamed of."

He looked at me.

"The house will be quiet. Maybe you can think and relax a little."

He started the engine, then turned to me once more.

"Two things. I didn't have anything to do with Grandpa's death. You should know that without me saying it."

I took that in and stared at the ground.

"And two?" I asked.

"The upstairs room is yours, if you ever want to share it with someone. There are extra sheets in the closet."

22

As soon as Dad left I sat myself down with my scraps of newspapers. I found one with the bottom of a photo and a bit of credit line intact: "... Joy Constance Temp ..." It confirmed what I already suspected: I had had a photo in every *Times* issue Grandpa pulled out of his collection. He removed them but kept them. It was like he had to exorcise me, or his love for me, but couldn't, quite. Instead he stuck me where no one would think to look—except another Temper.

I went back through the Polaroids. I didn't admire the camera work. But they did what snapshots are supposed to do: delayed extinction and ignited memories.

When I was growing up, our house was a noisy place, full of people. Everyone worked together. At the end of the day everyone showered, often at the same time to save water, or washed off in the creek behind the property. We had no neighbors, no one to see or hear us. Then came dinner, wine, and weed. Our living room often turned into a communal bedroom, people huddled together in the colder winter months under large blankets, three or four bodies; or sprawled in nothing or not much more than underwear on the hot summer nights when even soft cotton rubbed like sandpaper. We all stripped down to essentials then: bras (not many of those that I remember), panties and t-shirts. Sometimes nothing at all. It might seem an odd childhood but then it was just who we were and how we lived.

As the only child, I was pampered, adored, taken care of—and privy to most everything. I got used to the sounds of sex—the whispered instructions, the sighs and cigarettes or arguments after. I got used to seeing men and women lying on top of each other, and what I later realized was the post-coital smell of sheets that didn't get washed often enough.

I would bring my Polaroid with me to the living room. I would photograph what I saw. Mostly quiet scenes. Tired from a day of work, Mom and Dad and their friends would sip a beer, drink wine, smoke, hold hands and talk. The men were often half-dressed, in briefs or boxers. The women were bare-chested like the men. When I wasn't in the living room I heard the adults talking and laughing from my bedroom, their voices a comforting lullaby.

Those were my memories, anyway. But now I could also see my life through Grandpa's eyes. The bare-chested women might have been enough to set him off. A few shots must have seemed more ominous. When I'm in a photo, it isn't always clear what I'm doing or who I'm with. There is one of me with my arms encircling a man's neck while he hugs me around the waist and holds me up high off the ground. My feet dangle at his thighs. I can see a penis sticking out between my ankles. Another two are of a naked man—Bobby I think—mugging a kiss on my toes, then on my knee. Uncle Thomas and Mom are holding me or near me in most of the other photos. In one I'm sitting on Uncle Thomas' lap. He's sitting on Mom's and she's on someone else. The adults are laughing. I can see bare arms and legs and can guess the rest. In other photos where I appear I'm in my pajamas—long in winter, shorts in summer—or just in underwear.

I stared at the pictures, looking for a hint of suppressed anxiety. Could I remember anything wayward, menacing or dangerous? The night I ran off, yes. I was terrified, frightened enough to have repressed the episode for three decades. But in the living room, surrounded by Dad, Mom, Uncle Thomas: all I saw looking back was love. Not the kind of love Dad and Mom and their friends might have declared would save the world in the 1960s and '70s, but love nonetheless. It was the messy kind that led me to Angie, that led Mom to Dad—that led to lies, grief, divorce, loss, and probably every discovery about ourselves worth discovering.

There was nothing in the photos that struck me as odd. The nights when these were taken weren't exceptional. Which I suppose might make them more horrifying to an outsider looking at them now. Or to Grandpa in 1979. The disorienting experience was realizing how safe I felt—and how certain I was that no one but the people who were there could believe that possible. Or maybe some people could. Angie could. Penny wouldn't want to.

23

I checked my phone to see if Angie had texted. Instead I found four voicemails from Mom. She was home from her month at Yosemite and no doubt expected me to be in San Francisco to welcome her. I wasn't looking forward to telling her about the last two weeks. Her tolerance for bullshit had declined with age.

It didn't take five minutes of my evasions for Mom to haul into me.

"What's really going on? Is your father OK?"

I laughed, then started to cry.

"Hold the tears, Joy. Please. You cry too much. They don't get us anywhere."

"Dad's fine," I sniffled. "He just left to drive back to Idaho."

"OK. One down. Now what aren't you saying?"

"Everything."

"Start."

I decided I'd kept my promise to Dad long enough. I told Mom about the funeral, Cheryl, and what I found at the China Mine. Penny I kept to myself.

There was a long silence on her end.

"Shit," she said finally. "Anyone else know about the dog tag?"

"Only Dad. He told me not to tell you," I added.

"Of course he did."

There was a pause. I think Mom covered the phone. She seemed to be talking to someone.

"OK. I've got to do some wash, then pack. I'll drive over tomorrow. That'll give you time to get the sheets and pillowcase on your bed cleaned."

Dramatic pause.

"I'm bringing Angie with me. She's sitting here sipping coffee and writing down directions to Temper so she can surprise you for your birthday. Act surprised."

Then she hung up.

My birthday. I'd forgotten. So had Dad, not for the first time.

What a celebration that was going to be.

1

It was mid-summer 1979 when the wheels came off—one at a time. None of what happened made sense to me. But my confusion didn't keep me from feeling that it was all my fault.

I got bored spending time with Grandpa. He slurred his words. More than once I had to scream him awake when we almost swerved into a car coming the other way on the narrow roads around Temper. I still liked to go to the store and see Grandma, and it was nice the way Grandpa counted on me to help with the bankbooks. But I spent more and more time with Uncle Thomas. We'd drive, pull over somewhere he knew about and wander.

We often wound up at the China Mine. That's where Grandpa found us. We were in the clearing above the mine looking at an arrowhead when Grandpa leaped out of the woods.

"Caught you, you aimless cuss!" he yelled, a baseball bat in his hand, rushing at Uncle Thomas in a zig-zag that told me Grandpa had been drinking. I never saw Uncle Thomas move so fast. He rolled away from me straight at Grandpa's legs and toppled him over onto his stomach. Then he jumped up, grabbed the baseball bat and held it by the handle, ready to bring it down on Grandpa, who was still lying there in shock. I ran over to Grandpa and helped him get to his hands and knees. Uncle Thomas stood by, alert.

"What are you doing to this child?" Grandpa yelled at Uncle Thomas.

Uncle Thomas didn't say a word. He stared at Grandpa. He looked so tired, as if he'd just come from hours of hard labor. He dropped the bat, turned, and started walking away. I yelled but Uncle Thomas never turned around. Soon he had disappeared into the brush.

Grandpa managed to stand, then staggered towards the bat. I got to it first.

"Give that to me," he ordered.

"No, Grandpa. Uncle Thomas didn't do nothing to me. He wouldn't hurt a wasp trying to sting him."

"Hard to believe the way he attacked me," Grandpa said, making another lunge for the bat while I backed a step away.

"Don't you let me ever see you up at this mine again, you hear me? Or with that moronic uncle of yours."

Uncle Thomas didn't come home that night or the next. I made Mom drive me up to the mine to look for him. He wasn't there. He showed up four days later, scraggly from sleeping out in the woods, and hungry. I asked him where he had been. All he would say was,

"Talking to the ghosts."

When I tried to bring up what happened, he shook his head at me, took my hand, and held it softly until I stopped asking questions.

2

Two days later, Grandma Alice drove up to our house. She talked to Mom and Dad and told me to get my backpack and come with her back to town. I'd stay for dinner, do my homework, and then she would bring me home.

"Your grandfather is a cranky old man who can't ever say he's wrong, child," she said to me on the way. "We need to be the ones."

"I wasn't wrong, Grandma. Neither was Uncle Thomas," I said.

"I know that, but Isaac never will. Just come into the store with me. We can play cards at the counter. Isaac will watch us for a while then ask you to help him with the bank accounts and it will all be over."

Grandma was half right. We played cards while Grandpa took care of customers and pretended not to notice the two of us. Around four, he asked if I would help him with the accounts.

They didn't add up. I redid the figures and recounted the money. There were always eleven dollars missing. Grandpa made me redo everything again and again until it was clear that some of the money that had been noted had either not been deposited, or had been deposited and now was gone.

Grandpa got up, paced back and forth as if thinking, then stood over me where I was sitting with the dollar bills in a pile on my lap.

"Where did you hide the money, Joy? This isn't a game. You don't have to steal," Grandpa said, moving to my side.

"I didn't take the money, Grandpa. You know I'd never do that."

He started to walk away then turned back suddenly.

"Now I get it. He put you up to this. To get back at me. Well I'll see that he gets what he deserves. Just tell me it was his fault."

What Grandpa said made no sense. I stood up, angry.

The dollar bills flew all over the floor. Grandpa didn't give them a second look. Instead he reached in his pocket and took out a stack of silver dollars. He held them up to me.

"Is this what he wanted? We have the evidence. He can be in jail tonight."

I didn't understand what was happening.

"I didn't steal," I screamed. "Uncle Thomas didn't ask me to. It's you!"

I ran at Grandpa, screaming: "I didn't take your money. You know I didn't. I didn't." He grabbed one of my wrists and seemed to pull his fist hand back, like he was going to hit me. I lifted up one foot and stomped on his toes, then raised my knee between his legs. He screamed and let go for an instant. I ran past him and out the door. I kept running, down the street, onto Bitter Root Road and all the way home. Mom was in the kitchen along with Amy and Gwen. I was panting, tears running down my face. They rushed over. I hugged Mom and blubbered, "I didn't do it. I didn't do it. He's wrong. He made it up. He wants to hurt Uncle Thomas." It took a few minutes and Mom's lap for me to quiet enough to tell the story. By that time, Dad and Preacher were listening too.

I turned to Dad.

"I didn't take that money, Daddy. Honest. I swear. He had it in his hand. Grandpa had it in his hand and he wanted to blame Uncle Thomas and me."

"We know. You told us, Joy. Grandpa was playing a trick on you, a mean trick."

"Why would he do that?"

"I don't know. But you are not going back there. We'll find other ways to let you have time with Grandma."

That turned out to be another wrong prediction.

3

After Grandpa published some of my photos in the *Times*, I decided to bring him the pictures I was taking at home— daytime shots of us working on the house, and photos of Mom and Dad and our friends. They all went together: this was my life. I wanted Grandpa to know that, to know that he didn't need to stay mad at Dad.

I put all the photos in my backpack. They sat there, for- gotten, buried beneath my books, school papers, and the scrunched-up wax paper Mom used to wrap my sand- wiches. How long did I carry them around—days? weeks? Did some instinct make me hesitate? If so, it was a good one.

I woke up to pounding at the front door. By the time I got into the hall Grandpa was standing just inside the doorway, my backpack in one hand, the other holding my Polaroids.

He raged into the house. Dad tried to put himself in

Grandpa's path but Grandpa pushed by him. It was Preacher who stopped him at the living room entry. I walked over, still groggy, and stood behind Grandpa. Preacher had put jeans on but Amy and Bobby, Gwen and Charlie were slower, dressed in a mix of bra (Gwen), boxers (Bobby), a mostly unbuttoned blouse without a bra (Amy), and jeans barely up to his knees (Charlie), his penis swinging side to side as he struggled into them.

Grandpa turned around and saw me craning into the doorway. He yelled, dropped the backpack, grabbed my head and put his hand over my eyes.

"Don't look!" he said to me.

At that point, Dad came over, pulled Grandpa's hand off me, and moved back a step, holding me to him. He was only wearing his boxers and seemed like he was shivering. Mom had disappeared. Then I saw her come down the stairs dressed in a t-shirt and cut-offs. She stopped a few steps above us.

"Isaac," she yelled.

When Grandpa didn't make a move she screamed at him again.

"Isaac!"

He turned.

"Shameful woman!" he yelled.

"Stop it," she yelled back. "You don't come into my house in the middle of the night for no reason."

"Reason? No reason?"

He swung his arm back towards the living room and extended the other, with the pile of photos, at Mom.

"Here's my reason. A whorehouse. A whorehouse in my town."

Grandpa seemed about to rush up the stairs at Mom but Preacher got him in a bear hug. Grandpa yelled and tried to move, but no one moved when Preacher didn't want them to.

"Isaac, get out of here. Now," Mom said. "Whatever you have to say to us will wait until morning."

"Not on your life, you miserable creature. Letting my granddaughter live in this filth. Nakedness, sex, incest, sodomy!"

Mom's face exploded. She ran down the last steps and slapped Grandpa across the face. Then she swung at him with the other hand. She was about to slap him again when Dad grabbed her arm, held her from behind, and stared over her at Grandpa.

"Go," is all he said.

"I'll not leave that child in this house another night."

"Nonsense," Dad said, his voice so quiet he might have been talking to himself. He let go of Mom, stood in front of her, and pulled at the pile of photos in Grandpa's hand. Some went flying, but Grandpa kept hold of most of them.

"Harriet and I will come to your house after we drop Joy off at school," Dad said, almost nose to nose with Grandpa. "I want Ma there too."

"I ain't leaving without the rest of the evidence," Grandpa said, looking at the photos on the floor. Then he screamed into Dad's face:

"All of this, this filth. You've come here, corrupted your friends and polluted the ground. You and my father. Leaving you this land. You're no Temper and never were."

Dad didn't flinch.

"When I look at you, I wish I wasn't," he said.

He glanced at the photos scattered around them.

"We'll bring these with us."

He nodded to Preacher, who dragged Grandpa down the hall and out the door.

Next day, Mom picked me up after school. Dad was waiting for the two of us with cookies and lemonade. I looked at Dad, ran to him and buried my head in his lap. He put his hand on my hair and pulled at it gently for a moment. Then he had me stand up straight so I could see his face.

"Grandpa is wrong about us and our friends, you know that?"

I nodded.

"But—," he started.

He stopped and looked up at Mom. She came over and let me lean on her.

"Tommy needs to go away," she said.

"Why?" I asked.

"Because of your grandfather."

"But he's wrong. Grandpa's wrong. You said so. Uncle Thomas never hurt me. We never stole any money."

It was Dad's turn.

"We do know that, Joy. We can't explain why. He just has to."

"Where is he?" I asked, suddenly frightened.

"He's already gone. He said to tell you goodbye and to take care of the ghosts for him."

"I don't believe you."

I ran to Uncle Thomas' room. It was empty. The sheets were off the bed, the closet a bunch of loose hangers. I ran back into the kitchen.

"Where is he? Where did he go?"

Dad tried to hug me but I swung back and forth angrily until he let go.

"You can't see him, Joy. He's on a bus to San Francisco."

"When is he coming back?"

Dad looked at Mom. She stood holding on to the kitchen counter, like she couldn't stand up on her own.

"He's not coming back. Not to Temper," Mom said.

I ran at Mom and started banging my fists on her. She didn't protect herself, but Dad came up behind me and held my arms.

"Stop, Joy. This is not what we wanted either."

I turned around then, looked up at Dad, and somehow knew for sure that it was true. I started to cry huddled against him.

I don't remember what happened the rest of that day. The next morning I woke up in my bed. The house was silent. I found Mom in the kitchen smoking a cigarette. I went up to her and she gave me a hug. Dad was gone somewhere in the truck. No one else was around.

I didn't go to school the rest of that week. I see-sawed between screaming at Mom and Dad and crying in their arms. None of their friends ever came to the house again, except Preacher. I didn't ask where they went or why. I knew it had to do with the pictures and Grandpa. And knew enough to bury what I knew.

4

Life turned quiet at home. Dull. I went to school, did my homework, helped Dad with little building projects and Mom with the garden. We stopped growing and selling weed. That meant Dad had to get more jobs away from home to make money.

That's how Cheryl Moreland came into our lives—just a name over dinner, someone who hired Dad to add an office to a house she owned in the first large (for Temper) housing development on the east side of town. Cheryl was one of the investors. Dad had worked on most of the houses, so it made sense for her to ask him to supervise her add-on. Or that's what Mom and I thought.

It was mid-July, just before my ninth birthday, when Cheryl came for dinner. She was sitting at the picnic table on our deck when I stormed up and stuck a scorpion in her face.

She tried to jump back, got herself tangled between the bench and the top of the table and started falling towards me. She put up her hand, pushed at my shoulder and righted herself with a screech.

"Aren't those things poisonous?" she cried.

She wore dark lipstick and smelled. Perfume, which I didn't have much experience with. Chanel No. 5 I learned when she and Dad got married and I started my summer visits to her houses.

"It won't bite," I told her.

Cheryl pulled back farther and turned to my mother. "Don't they sting?"

"Not her," Mom explained. "Prenatal vaccine. I got stung on my belly when I was about six months pregnant. I woke up feeling like someone had stuck a pointed scrap of wood into me. I felt it scampering along my tummy and yelled. David woke up and swept it onto the floor."

Mom explained me that way. I was immune, protected from the womb.

"Those are dangerous, whatever you say," Cheryl insisted. "You should get her a dog, something she can run around and play with. Wouldn't you like a dog?" she asked me.

I was still holding the scorpion. I didn't like dogs. When I was five, three hounds were lying on the porch of Grandpa's store when I came by after school. They started to bark, circled, sniffed the air, and inched towards me.

I froze. Their owners called them back. The hounds hesitated, looking to each other for guidance, and reluctantly obeyed, turning away. But the damage was done. I had peed down my overalls. I stood like that until Grandma Alice came out of the store, took my hand and led me inside.

From then on I ran from any dog that tried to get friendly. I didn't need a pet; I had a whole woods full of them.

Scorpion still in hand, I turned away from Cheryl and back towards the house.

Dad was turning meat, eggplants and peppers on the grill. I started to drop the scorpion onto the woodpile where I'd found it, then changed my mind, found an empty Mason jar and lid, and stuck the scorpion in there. I hid the jar in my bedroom.

I headed off behind the house and climbed up the roof of the A-frame to the deck outside Mom and Dad's bedroom. I let myself in, walked through and into the upstairs hall. From there I could look down on Mom and Cheryl sitting at the table outside the sliding glass doors.

Mom was scratching at her arm just above the elbow, the way she does still when she's upset. Cheryl was sipping at something in her glass. I couldn't hear what they were saying. It was pantomime, TV with the sound off.

Dad came up with the food. Mom went inside. Cheryl reached a hand across the table to Dad. He didn't take it—just busied himself cutting up the meat. Cheryl stood up, reached toward Dad again, and brushed her fingers down his arm. That was when Mom came out. I saw her drop silverware down on the table and stare off at the driveway.

I went downstairs to my own bedroom, grabbed the blanket off my bed and the Mason jar. I walked back upstairs and stood in the hall, feeling invisible. No one noticed that I wasn't around or seemed to care. I walked down again, out the front door and over to Cheryl's car, a red convertible. The top was down, so it was easy to open the

Mason jar and drop the scorpion onto the driver's seat. Then I went to the back of the house, climbed back up to Mom and Dad's bedroom, and went over to their closet. Their clothes, dirty and clean, were on the floor as usual. I burrowed in the way I did with leaves in the forest—the way I did, often, when I knew something was wrong but not what. And went to sleep.

I woke when I heard Mom yelling. "I'm meatloaf?" "You can split logs with one of those heels." I heard Dad ask Mom to quiet down. I heard him say, "You'll wake Joy." Mom really let loose then. Something slammed into a wall, fell to the floor and smashed. Mom pulled open the closet door. I peeked my head out of the clothes and smiled.

A horn started blaring. I heard tires screech to a stop and Cheryl scream outside in front of the house. Dad rushed downstairs. Mom looked at me and started crying so I hugged her leg.

Dad came back after a few minutes. He saw me attached to Mom just below the knee. He unhooked my arms, picked me up, and carried me to my room. I was still dressed and still hadn't eaten. He covered me, turned out the light and closed the door. I lay there clutching the covers over my ears to blot out Mom and Dad yelling at each other until I fell asleep. Nothing more was ever said about that night, and I never asked.

It was maybe a week after Cheryl's arrival that Dad came home with the dog. Mom didn't say anything while he walked up from the car with the excited animal in his arms. I ran behind Mom for protection.

"Very nice, David," Mom said. "But why didn't you just buy Joy a Barbie doll so she could dress it up to look like Cheryl?"

Dad ignored her, held the dog by a collar around its neck and brought it closer to me. I put a hand out to its wet nose and let it lick my palm. Then I tried touching its back but it zipped its head around to nip at my hand. I bolted straight for my room. The dog yanked out of Dad's grasp and caught up with me before I could close my bedroom door. I jumped onto my bed and covered myself until Dad grabbed the animal, pulled it away and shut the door.

The dog was gone by dinner. Mom had locked herself in her room and wouldn't answer when I knocked. Dad made me a peanut butter and jelly sandwich, helped me brush my teeth, and got me into bed. I watched through the window as he drove off in his truck.

I don't know when he came home. I woke to hear Mom screaming at him from the top of the stairs.

"You're not coming a step closer! Enough is enough. Go back to your vampire and let her suck the blood out of you."

Dad must have slammed the front door and pounded down the deck stairs. Mom ran after him. She threw a beer bottle or two—the glass was still in the front yard the next morning. Mom's friend Clare drove up from Los Angeles in her pickup the next day. We slept in a motel that night. Mom whispered back and forth with Clare. I was on a cot across the room. Next day we came back for our clothes and headed down to Los Angeles. Mom, Clare and I celebrated my ninth birthday a few days later at Clare's apartment—three cupcakes, mine with a candle.

1

It took Mom and me four years from the night we left Temper to find our way to her family in San Francisco: six months with Clare in L.A., Fresno for ten, and Sacramento the rest of that time.

I barely remember Los Angeles. I spoke in monosyllables and mumbled words. When Dad called, Mom described me as catatonic, my development truncated by the separation. My teacher wanted to exile me to Special Ed.

Fresno was a townhouse we shared with Anna, Mom's college roommate: a single mom raising a seven-year-old named Whitney who swiped anything of mine he could. Mom worked at a childcare center. I started to talk again, but woke screaming at night from bad dreams.

Fresno ended suddenly. When I ran into the kitchen one morning, Mom had cardboard boxes on the table, some already sealed. Anna was helping her wrap the few dishes we owned in paper. Mom's left eye was puffed and purple, her cheeks red. There was a bandage across her jaw. When I rushed up to her she gave me a long hug, then set me at arm's length in front of her so she could look me in the eye.

"If you think this is bad, you should see the other guy. Collect your clothes and anything else you don't want to leave behind. Say goodbye to Whitney and do not take any of his toys! Make a pile in the living room."

I nodded and ran back to the room Whitney and I shared. I wanted to cry but didn't want him to see I was upset. I went through my drawers, grabbed piles of clothes and books, and threw everything I could find on the pile. Whitney watched, came over, and stuck a pair of his dice in my hand. And that was Fresno.

Sacramento was quieter. We rented a small house. Mom worked at a fabric store and then found a job at a yarn shop. She managed to be home nights and weekends. The neighbors were older than her. Their houses had tiny grass yards in front and back yards with tall wooden fences and concrete patios. I went to school, made friends, was bored and hot in the summers and got into enough fights to keep Mom screaming at me. Vacations were a week at Lake Tahoe in a rented cabin.

Sacramento was when Mom settled down. Got set in her ways, the crowd in Temper would have said. She bought a used TV and would sit in front of it nights, yarn moving through her fingers while Reagan succeeded Carter and people whispered about AIDS, Iran-Contra, and Star Wars—none of which interested me at the time.

Mom started crocheting afghans. She's always crocheting, the yarn a tail she drags along. She crochets through conversations, confessions, dinner parties, and election results. Through 9/11, Afghanistan, the fall of Iraq, the recession. Pulling, knotting. Winding and unwinding the yarns. Counting the rows of stitching, the colors and the flower patterns she inserts with an ease that looks less like work than, say, turning one page after another of a magazine.

Mom's father died in 1984. I didn't know her family well. Mom carried me back to Chicago once, right after we moved to Temper. The apartment we stayed in was small and filled with kitchen smells. It was on the fourth floor with a back porch where you could see the garbage cans below and wave at the trains as they went by. It was hot and sticky—it felt even hotter than Temper. I saw my first fireflies. That was about all the experience I had with my granddad, Granny Eva and Aunt Jane—that visit and moments on the phone when they would ask if I'd found any snakes or scorpions to play with.

Granny Eva and Aunt Jane sold their house and used that money along with Granddad's life insurance to buy a place in the Haight. I still don't know why. "To get away from winter" is what Granny said when I asked. "To see if the drugs out there are as good as they say" was Aunt Jane's explanation. "To spend time with you" was Mom's glib lie when I complained that I didn't want to leave Sacramento, which wasn't true.

Mom and I moved to a converted storage shed out back of Granny's house. We shared a loft bedroom created by curtains strung between partial walls. Downstairs there was an electric double burner, tiny refrigerator and sink, and a ladder to the loft. There was no bathroom, so we crossed the stubby lawn to one in the house. I learned to love that shed—the climb up and down the ladder, the pipes and hooks where we hung clothes, the plywood floors and unvarnished beams.

Granny had worked at Marshall Fields in Chicago so she quickly found a job selling jewelry at Macy's. She spent her nights sitting with a glass of white wine in her hand, her legs up on a footstool in front of the bay window. Aunt Jane worked for Macy's too, in accounting. She found the drugs she wanted and moved haphazardly back and forth between AA and NA meetings. There were relapses—a lot of them, notable for rants about blacks, the gays who were taking over the city and the liberals who were screwing up the country. Her commentaries soon became white noise, that hint of static on the car radio you can't quite get rid of.

Granny got sick the fall I started college. Aunt Jane took away Granny's wine and made her get out of bed to walk the long hallway five or six times a day. She refused to let the doctors ease up on care when it was clear that all that was left were a few strained breaths before Granny would die.

A wiry man named Zachary Nathan appeared at the funeral. He introduced himself to Mom and Aunt Jane at the house after, passing around his business cards.

"I met your mother at Macy's, dear lady. She had the eye for diamonds and I will forever be grateful for her kindness. Years and years of it, finding pieces for my wife. I helped your mother with a will. It seemed the least I could do."

They stared at him like he was speaking Martian.

"I hope we can find time soon to meet together and consider its contents."

Then he took a few nuts in his hand and slipped out.

Jane was apoplectic, swearing her mother would never consort with a Jew. A week later Mom told me that Granny had left the house to her. The furniture, her old car and about $10,000 in the bank went to Jane.

Jane accused Mom of tricking Granny. Mom hired an attorney. Jane hired a detective and put him on Uncle Thomas' trail, hoping that he would want the money, side with her, and tip the scales of justice. The detective came up empty: Uncle Thomas was nowhere to be found and the house went to Mom.

2

Once I left Temper, I left Dad. Or he left me. He was never out of my life, but not much in it either. The divorce thing—summer visits, birthday and Christmas presents, calls when he remembered. The calls usually included Mom arguing with him over missed childcare payments, which really meant Cheryl.

Cheryl wanted to reform me. Nothing about me was suitable—her word. She took me shopping, made appointments for me at the beauty parlor, taught me to sit up, keep elbows down, chew more slowly and not talk with food in my mouth. I set the dinner table so I'd learn where to put the silverware and how to fold cloth napkins.

As the years went by Cheryl found that I wasn't any more gracious or polite and less and less pliable. I turned up with scraped elbows and dirty fingernails, tears in the blouses, rips in the skirts and unmatched socks. I developed a distaste for dresses and found a way to stain the ones Cheryl insisted I wear. Spaghetti sauce worked well, salad dressing better. A few times I peed on them. I snuck into Cheryl's closet and stole silk scarves I took home with me so Mom and I could use them for rags. It was my revenge. Whether I was getting revenge for myself or for Mom I never stopped to ask.

My visits with Cheryl and Dad were a boot camp in passive resistance: a studied if unconscious strategy that I couldn't label until college psychology courses. I didn't know I had it in me until then and didn't even think to examine the whys. It was only later, as I learned to live with Angie and she called me on my moods that I realized how much resentment went into everything I did and said those years.

Mostly I missed Dad, my dad, the one I loved and wanted to love me. Finally, with the move to San Francisco, I begged Mom not to make me go anymore. Mom was easy to draw into the conspiracy. So no Dad until he and Cheryl divorced.

———————

Did Dad leave Cheryl, or Cheryl throw him out? All I remember is the phone call when he told me. They were together five years. That means four summer visits, adding up to less than three months of actual days. Not exactly Cinderella's forced labor. Looking back, I realize I was as awful to Cheryl as she was to me, or worse. Even admitting my complicity in my misery, I have spent most of my life hating her. And Dad too, a bit, for loving her or whatever he called it. I've never found much comfort in retrospect.

I thought I'd given up on Dad. I realize now I wouldn't have been so defiant if I had. When Dad would leave me at Mom's door I would go to bed and lie there, staring up at the ceiling, a vacant feeling in my bones, like I'd failed him. The pride I had in my acting out disappeared in his absence. But I knew too that he'd failed me in some way I couldn't name. I was more alone after our times together than before.

When I was eighteen, Dad moved to Boise and met Madge in the camera store she owned. It was love at first pixel, Dad liked to say. He settled in where he seemed to belong. He gave me his camera, a heavy Nikon that I lugged all over, from college to work, friends' birthday parties to Europe. I started shooting alongside him in summers. It was the only camera I owned until I turned twenty-five and moved to digital.

My college years were the best times with Dad. By then I didn't need or want a full-time father, so our infrequent phone calls and the summer week or two we'd both reserve for each other were enough. He had a business, access to all the camera equipment he would ever need, and a daily life with someone he loved. Madge didn't like to travel and hated car trips. She was happy to stay home and care for the store while Dad and I wandered. It was just the two of us, camping and shooting pictures. We'd go all over the west—California, Nevada, Idaho, Oregon, Montana, Colorado. I'd bring along my year's photos for him to critique and he'd offer advice about framing and lighting.

Traveling with Dad was a process of sudden starts and stops. He drove with his heart on the brakes, ready to pull over the instant he got some hint of a subject in his mental viewfinder. He would turn off to photograph artichokes outside Castroville, an abandoned archway of a deserted house somewhere in Half Moon Bay. He moved on to silos—old and new, metal or wood, in use or a worn relic with missing slats. Silos gave way to stairways, steep ones at the edge of an abandoned house, partially disassembled stringer boards and risers in someone's yard, or railroad ties placed across a forest trail.

I didn't share Dad's love for abandoned things. I used to walk around San Francisco focusing on doorknobs, knockers, and bells. When I traveled with Dad I shifted to parts of animals—a pig's snout, a cow's ear hanging down, a horse's leg or the knob at the joint. I took close-ups of lamb fleece, a bull's horn, a wolf's paw a farmer had on his mailbox by the side of the road. And I had a thing for fences—metal, barbed wire, split rail, dry stonewalls. We barely noticed the bluffs and gorges, mountains and lengths of river that we'd drive by. I came to appreciate the way Dad packed a car, set up a tent, and made a fire. I'd get the sleeping bags ready, start dinner, and pull out a book. I loved his quiet. The only complaints I ever heard from him were an occasional moan when he'd stand up suddenly after bending too long, followed by the same dismissive line:

"Getting old," he'd say, and smile at me.

"Better than not," I'd answer.

A lot of love in those words.

I saw more lines on his face, but not many. His lanky frame and easy gait were the first things Angie mentioned to me when she met him, more than a year after we moved in together.

3

Angie entered my life on a hot August afternoon in 1997. I was in Venice with Kate and Helen, two college roommates who'd morphed into best friends and traveling companions. They were exhausted and eager to catch up on sleep after a long night on the train, bus, and vaporetto. I grabbed my camera and headed to Piazza San Marco to see if I could find cooler air near the water. Angie and I were standing next to each other in a small group of tourists. We were both staring up—she shielding her eyes from the setting sun, me behind my viewfinder struggling to take a decent photo against the increasing shadows. Then some sneering Italian men did what sneering Italian men do—the hissing intake of breath, the whistles and catcalls.

I'd been hearing the noises for days—in Rome and Florence, on trains, buses and street corners. But I was alone this time. I dropped the camera back around my neck, turned around and held up my middle finger. So did the woman next to me. She was tall, with braided hair. We looked at each other and laughed, while the men laughed back at us, unashamed, proud even, and ready with louder hisses.

Angie says she was in love in minutes, her eyes lost in my short hair and smile. I've never been famous for my smile—braces didn't quite cure my cross-bite—but I want to believe her. It took me longer to realize what was going on—two weeks, four countries, and a lot of nudges from Kate and Helen longer. At first she was just Angie, a stranger I started talking to wearing one of those small leather backpack-handbags I find so silly. It seemed particularly minuscule on her long, broad back. We drank overpriced and underhopped Italian beers at one of the cafés and agreed we'd find each other early the next morning. She moved to our pension. Kate and Helen took to her. She was easy, fun, and alone.

Angie was from Cleveland, which I learned meant four different rural towns spotted over Ohio before she settled in what was for her the big city for college then business school. She was already a foodie. She took notes about everything from menus to tourist snacks. She was unabashed, mixing bad Italian, some English and hand signals to ask questions. Because of her I ate fish I never learned the names of, walked into *osterias* I would have ignored, found myself exclaiming about the taste of octopus and eel, snails and gizzard stews. She opened up a Europe—a life—I never dreamed of until then.

Angie was moving across the continent from east to west. Kate, Helen and I were traveling in the opposite direction. She abandoned her plans and joined us until Athens, when Kate and Helen headed for a few days of play in Mykonos and left the two of us alone with encouraging glances. We went to Meteora and kissed in the shadowy walkway of a cloister with the precipitous mountains below. It was the first time I kissed a woman. I mean *really* kissed a woman. I loved the way our chests grazed, the movement of her hand along the length of my abdomen. Angie was just a touch taller than me, bigger breasted and not as narrow-hipped. Our similar size let us lean comfortably against each other, cheek along cheek. We stood for a long time in that doorway. Our hands moved slowly over back, neck, and hair, indifferent to glances from passers-by. We separated, walked hand in hand up the stairways, through the monasteries, and back to our room in Kastraki. We found our way from there to Olympia and Mani, where the heat left us limp in each other's arms. We fell in love with the towers and old smokestack in Kardamili, walked the bone-dry gorge, and swam to cool our sunburned skin. The dry landscape, the warm winds and the incessant heat intensified our desires. We surrendered to the sand and dust. When we met Helen and Kate again in Athens, they laughed at the way we blushed, felt for the other's hand, insisted on contact along an arm, elbow or shoulder. They hugged us goodbye and traveled on as originally planned to Turkey. I flew to Dublin with Angie. We left London the same day on separate flights—she to pick up her clothes in Cleveland, quit her job, sell her furniture and meet me in San Francisco.

I was living with Mom when Angie arrived. Life was good, then perfect when Angie came. We found our apartment upstairs of a gay couple—Sal and Larry—who had just bought and remodeled the building. They were ecstatic about Angie's offer to turn the weedy backyard into a garden.

Those first months were astonishing, and simple: the discovery, morning after morning, of this face on the pillow next to mine, curious to know what was next. Her hands were better than lotion to me. We tag-teamed our way through the Sunday crossword puzzle, climbed Mt. Tamalpais in the rain. We cleaned the apartment, scrubbed toilets and bathtubs. By the time we were done with the tub we were nuzzling. It wasn't all sex. It might be a long kiss, a hand running down the back as we crossed along the hallway, or leaning into each other in our narrow kitchen.

Angie quickly found a job reviewing applications at the local American Culinary Institute. Admissions gave way to low-level management. Then four years ago she uncovered a scam that had cost the Institute $240,000. She didn't make a lot of friends locally blowing the whistle, but she was magic with the national office in Virginia. And so began her travel, sweeping into one cooking school after another, redesigning the allotments, the loan procedures, and the sign-off process. She uncovered fake accounting entries and other scams that saved ACI tens of thousands of dollars. She spent her off time with the staff learning how to cook and making ink drawings and watercolor paintings of food, plates, copper pots, and kitchen tools.

When Angie got off the plane that August twelve years ago she gave me a late birthday present: a glass doorknob. She found it in a junk shop in Cleveland where she went to sell her furniture. She remembered the photos I was taking of doors, windows, knobs, and handles all through Europe. The rust and divots that made the knobs inoperable only emphasized the glistening glass facets.

And doorknobs it's been ever since. She's given me eleven of them so far—each different, all glass. They are as various as the years we've spent together: six, eight, and twelve facets; opaque white, robin's egg blue, green, and clear crystal. They're all chipped one place or another. They sit in a bowl on the coffee table in the living room at our apartment. I love to fidget with them, move the colors and shapes around, and turn and twist the mechanisms.

Angie's first oil paintings were of doorknobs. She'd choose one of my photos and paint from that. She does square canvases, 9x9, in pastel hues, with flat backdrops. Diffuse reflections spot the glass. We've mounted her paintings along the hallway side by side with my photos of the same doorknob—my high contrast black and white prints and my more recent color photos alternating with her delicate, precise but subdued versions. We showed them together at the SF Culinary Institute for a month, then at the Holy Bean, our local coffee house. People wanted to buy them but I wouldn't part with any. That twinning was an endless confirmation for me—my photos and her paint, my black and whites and her pastels, my bright primaries and her washes.

4

Until. I want to believe that there doesn't have to be an until—that sometime in my life there won't be an until except the death-do-us-part one.

I knew that Angie had been in love before, with women who came out to visit and stayed with us for a few days or a week. They hugged me and told me how happy it made them to see Angie happy. They brought their lovers with them, who also hugged me and smiled, drank our wine and bought some to leave with us before they left.

But I kept imagining Angie in some kitchen, meeting a chef who made perfect soufflés and rolled filo dough so fine it caught between your teeth. It didn't help that Angie came home to me, wanted me, and took over the kitchen for days after a trip trying out a tagine or wild mushroom and parsnip soup. There was always the next trip ahead, the next weeks alone and the next kitchen to worry about, where some curly blonde hair might reveal itself just so.

Until a few years went by and I noticed I took Angie's departures almost in stride. I assumed Angie would come home. My jealousy lapsed. I stopped wondering who the Angie would be who walked through the door. It was Angie, always Angie. Then it was just Angie—the woman I loved, lived with, and who loved me; who liked dark clothes and empty rooms and quiet; who liked toothpaste rolled from the bottom, leftovers in jars and socks folded in pairs. Angie-who-gave-a-finger-to-the-Italians had morphed into this other woman. Joy-who-gave-a-finger-to-the-Italians had morphed too.

The movies and soaps have it wrong: we don't notice change in what we do so much as what we stop doing. Angie liked to stay up late, I went to bed early. When she slid into the sheets there was no arm stretching over to grab my hand or weave our fingers together. And I didn't extend mine to her. I used to love how she would push against me, how I would lift myself and hover over her face until she reached up for a kiss. Then I stopped and she stopped. Or she stopped and I stopped. We went to sleep.

When the alarm rang in the morning I would get out of

bed, turn on the coffee maker, shower, dress, pour the coffee, cook the oatmeal and cut up fruit. Angie would grab an extra fifteen minutes of sleep, sip the coffee and head to her meditation pillow. Then we exchanged rushed "I love yous," along with "Are you stopping for food or should I?" as I ran out the door. She made the bed, cleaned the dishes, dried them, put them away and scoured the sink.

The process was efficient, the product of years of attention, followed by years of inattention. I didn't keep a chart, so it's anecdotal, this feeling of more and more of less and less. I would leave the cap off the toothpaste, drop my clothes in the hallway, or cover the bathroom counter with jewelry and perfume bottles. Angie would cap the paste, pick up the clothes and reorganize the bracelets, earrings and perfumes. Her outfits—black on gray on black on black on dark blue—started to look like penitentiary gowns hanging in the closet or on her. I got used to the way she beelined from doorway to stereo and shut off the Elvis Costello or X I was listening to, replacing Cervenka with Torme, Kroll, or Nat King Cole. What *is* the right word for that slacking off—the daily disappointments, the forgetfulness, the more and more frequent beg-pardons of love?

PART

V

1

After hanging up with Mom I stripped the sheets off my bed and realized the only way to wash them was how Mom and Dad used to when we lived here—soak them in the bathtub, empty the dirty water and rinse, rinse again, and again.

I set them out to dry on clotheslines Dad had restrung behind the house. I took a walk to town, turned around and walked home. The trip left me where I started—afraid to see Angie, ashamed that I'd let Grandpa get hold of the Polaroids. The sun had dried the sheets. I made the bed in my room, lugged my stuff upstairs to Dad's. After a salad and wine I got in the bathtub myself, slipped into the hot water, and fell asleep. It was almost midnight when I woke up. The minute I did I realized who was living at the mine.

It was easy to find the clearing again. I circled out from there but saw nothing. I went back to the mineshaft and slowly moved my flashlight beam around the walls. The blanket and duffel bag were gone. I went back to the clearing.

"Uncle Thomas. It's Joy. Come talk to me."

I repeated myself, stopped and listened. The cicadas quieted for an instant each time I called.

After fifteen minutes I shifted my plea.

"Mom is coming tomorrow. She knows you're here."

The third time I repeated those words I heard his voice. He was near me, behind my back.

"Why, Miss Why?"

I turned around. He had appeared without making a sound. He looked thin, his once broad chest collapsed, his arms frail. He had a scraggly mustache and beard, with bits of food visible around his mouth. His hair was matted and greasy. He wore a long-sleeved flannel shirt, the tails hanging over his jeans. No socks, no laces on his leather shoes.

"Why what, Uncle?"

"Why is your mother coming?"

"To see you. To help if she can."

"She always was one for trying to help."

I walked closer. He didn't pull back or move forward.

"It has been so long," I said to him. "I've missed you."

"I'm always here. I carry you with me."

"But I've missed our walks. I've missed holding your hand."

"I can't see you. The light," he said to me.

I turned it off. That left me blind.

"Tell her hello. I don't want to burden no one. No one, no more. Not her, not your father."

The words seemed to come from farther off. When I flicked the light back on he was gone. I flashed it into the surrounding trees but I couldn't find him. I turned the flashlight off and he spoke again.

"I never meant no harm. Say that to her, your mom."

"She already knows that, Uncle Thomas."

"Tell your father too. I was afraid to tell him."

"There's nothing to be afraid of with Dad. He loves you."

"I know that. I love you all."

"Can I bring you anything?" I asked.

I got no answer, heard no noise. I could have been there alone but knew I wasn't.

I found my way back to the mine, took the necklace Penny gave me out of my pocket, unhooked the dog tag, and laid the chain on a rock where I hoped Uncle Thomas might find it. Then I got in the car and drove home. It was only when I stood in the kitchen that I thought back to Uncle Thomas' comments about Dad. My confusions kept me awake longer than I wanted.

2

I woke to find that Penny had called twice. You home yet? Want to meet me somewhere for a drink? Are you OK?

No. No. No.

Avoiding Penny's calls was one thing, avoiding my confusion and anger another.

A man picked up on the first ring. Her roommate Alf. He yelled for her.

"Hey P! It's Goldirush." I heard a toilet flush, shoes banging on wood, then an exhale into the phone.

"You've been avoiding me," she said.

"Yes."

"What gives? You let me stew. You could have written something to tell me you didn't drown in the quarry."

"You're right."

"I know that. Tell me something I don't know."

"I've had other things on my mind. And I'm hurt and angry about the cemetery."

"That's a little better. It won't happen again, ever. I promise."

"I won't let it."

She paused. I heard her take a deep breath.

"I've been worried about you."

I had nothing to say to that.

"Trouble at home?"

"I'm expecting some."

"Bummer. Sorry. Really."

"Alf. Is he important to you?"

"We're roommates and have been for a long time."

"With benefits?"

"Some."

I waited.

"Why not? You didn't call or text. I'm involved here, you know?"

I still didn't say anything. Penny quieted.

"Can we talk? Can you come over?"

"No."

"Why?"

"Because I don't want to. And because I'm still in Temper."

"Why?"

"I'm trying to figure that out."

"It's not there, you know. What you want isn't there. Trust me."

"That didn't get me very far."

She laughed.

"Fair enough. But we have something, you and me. It could last. You know that."

"I used to," I admitted.

"But?"

"Exactly."

"You're not making sense, girl."

"I saw you were what I wanted. And now I see the 'buts' too."

"Like?"

"Like it took me years to get back here and I can't leave until I know why it took so long. Like my uncle might be in trouble. Like you don't get anything about this town or why it matters to me. Like my mom is on her way, along with Angie. Like I'm still in love with Angie. I can't walk away. Not now, not yet."

"She'll take you back and understand? You'll live happily ever, etc.?"

I didn't answer. I wasn't sure.

Penny stopped for a minute.

"Are you still wearing the necklace?"

"No. Do you want it back?"

"It's yours. Put it on the tracks if you don't want it. Let a train run over it."

"I told you. Temper never had a railroad station. It wasn't important enough."

"That's just what I've been telling you."

I laughed.

"I gave it to my uncle."

"The one you think is in trouble?"

"Yes."

"Maybe it will do him some good, help him cut and run the way you should."

"I doubt it," I told her.

"Then he's as doomed as you."

I paused for a moment.

"You might be right that Temper is not the place to find whatever it is I'm looking for. But chances are a lot better that I'll find it here than with you."

There was silence on Penny's end. A few seconds later she ended the call.

3

I couldn't sit waiting in the house any longer. I headed for the cemetery. I walked in on Preacher, his head and chest sticking out above a half-finished grave. He was wearing a pair of coveralls dark with dirt, helping two workmen prepare a new site. He laughed when he saw me.

"Caught in the act."

He dropped his shovel, talked to the men for a moment, then walked over to a hose and ran water over his hands. I waited for him on one of the paths.

"You do that often?" I asked.

"Pretty regularly. It's nice to get dirty. It helps me remember where the body goes when the soul departs. I dug part of Isaac's grave. With more relish than I should admit."

I remembered the way Preacher worked in the 1970s, hefting boards and beams larger than most of the men could carry and still with enough energy to serve me as horse, bucking bull, or surfboard before I went to bed.

"I'm glad to see you," he said.

He led me to the Temper family gravesites and began offering stories of one or another relative. I listened for a few minutes, then interrupted:

"Where are the Chinese buried? And the Mexicans?"

He looked at me as if he didn't understand the question.

"The ones who lived here in the Gold Rush. Who owned and worked the mines."

"If the family had money, they buried the dead in the Mission graveyards: San Juan Batista, San Jose, or San Francisco. Otherwise they were buried in one of the Catholic cemeteries nearby. Many were massacred in raids all over this region: who knows what happened to their remains? The Chinese who died of natural causes . . . they're mostly in China."

I looked confused.

"America was 'Gum san,' the Gold Mountain, but never home. Most Chinese men made sure their bodies would be shipped back to China. Others were disinterred in the last hundred years so their bones could be returned home."

Home.

I changed the subject.

"What can you tell me about forgiveness, Preacher?"

"Is that a conceptual or personal question?"

"Is anything conceptual?"

"I suppose not. The punishing God and the forgiving Son. Peter came to Jesus and asked how many times he should forgive. Seven? Jesus answered him: seventy-seven. That's Matthew. 'If you, O Lord, kept a record of sins, O Lord who could stand.' That's Psalms."

"And Preacher? What does Preacher say?"

"My struggle has mostly been to ask forgiveness, which is harder for me than to forgive. The people closest to you are the hardest to forgive, I think. Starting with yourself. I know that sounds New-Agey, but forgiveness starts at home."

He looked over to me. I started to blush.

I thought about Grandpa. Was I supposed to forgive him? He me? For what?

"It was because of my pictures that you and Bobby and the rest stopped coming to the house, right?"

He nodded.

"It was part of the deal David and Harriet made with Isaac. That and Tommy going."

"They traded for me."

"It wasn't a choice, Joy."

I nodded.

"But it must have hurt all of you. I'm sorry I didn't know any better."

"How could you? You were what—seven? eight? I'm sorry all of *us* didn't know any better."

We were quiet, walking side by side.

"You lost something those years, didn't you?" Preacher asked me. "I always wondered."

I started to tear up, sniffled instead.

"My parents, for one thing," I said. "This town. Safety. At least that's what I'm starting to think."

I stopped for a moment.

"There's this fracture, like a crack in the earth. It's a chasm I rarely cross."

"There's still time."

"I hope so," I said.

"One more thing," I went on. "Did Grandpa beat Dad? With a belt? And hurt Grandma Alice?"

Preacher nodded.

"I don't know much about your grandmother except

what David told me. But I saw David's back a few times after those lashings. Isaac could be ruthless when he thought he'd been crossed. You learned that yourself, didn't you?"

"I wonder if that's why he was so adamant about not selling out to Cheryl."

Preacher looked at me questioningly.

"It would have meant the end of his power around here. He told me once he was the last of the Mohicans. One day in this cemetery, in fact."

He looked at me—sadly I thought—thinking back.

"We're all better off without a tribe of Isaacs in the world."

4

Still restless, Penny still gnawing at me, I headed to the Inn for a beer and another look at the lake. It didn't seem as perfectly circular as the first time I saw it, or as magical as it became with Penny. It was water. It had receded from its banks in the summer heat. The lack of trees still oppressed me but I knew that with time the new ones the Inn had planted would reclaim the land. Or at least some of it.

Cheryl found me there, crying in my beer. She put a hand on my shoulder again, as she had that afternoon at the reception. I jumped again, startled. I didn't get up this time. She gently took her hand away when she saw my tear-stained face and offered me a handkerchief.

"Anything I can do?" she asked.

I shook my head. We sat like that while I sniffled, finished with the handkerchief, and handed it back.

"Do you own Temper General yet?" I asked.

"Not officially. The Sheriff's investigation got in the way. But I'm in no hurry."

I started to get up, then turned back to her.

"Do you know when Grandpa expected to start mining again?"

"Weeks ago, if you listened to him." she said. "He's been asking for permits from the City Council for months. People in town have told me that he's been going up to the mine almost every day the last weeks. Why?"

"I just wondered."

"Is your father still in town?" Cheryl asked.

"No. He left yesterday. I'm not sure when he'll be back." I turned to go.

"Love isn't easy," she said. "Maybe it's not meant to be."

"Tell me."

5

How do you welcome your mother into her former home that barely resembles where she used to live? Or your lover into a landscape she's only glimpsed in faded pictures and extravagant stories? You don't, I discovered, except by saying as little as possible, smiling back at their stares, preparing the dinner salad, opening the wine, and making sure not to mention Dad's double life, or mine. That worked until bedtime.

Dinner disappeared talking about Uncle Thomas.

"How did you know it was Tommy at the mine?" Mom asked me.

"There's no one else that would get you to rush into your car and return to Temper. At least that's what I figured."

"I would for you. Or your father."

"I'm glad to hear that. The dog tag tipped you off?" I asked.

She nodded.

"Tommy always carried one around in his pocket. It was his joke. No name, rank, serial number, blood type. After the Navy he was through with them."

"What happened to him?" Angie asked. She'd never met Uncle Thomas.

"I don't know exactly. The only thing Tommy would talk about was this moment when he was in a lifeboat—a drill of some kind. Someone he beat up in a boxing match pushed him overboard when he thought no one was looking. Tommy started to sink. A sailor in another boat jumped in and pulled him up.

"Tommy said that when he was in the water he just wanted to keep going down and never come back up. 'I wish they'd let me go,' he told me."

"He wasn't like that all the time he lived with us?" I asked to confirm my memories.

"No. He got along with folks. Until Isaac got in the way."

"It was because of me, my photos," I said.

Mom looked surprised.

I got up, went to the living room and grabbed the Polaroids. I shuffled through them, picked out a few, and handed them to Angie.

"I forgot them, or almost," I said to Mom.

"I've always wondered if you thought you were to blame."

Angie looked at the photos and passed them to Mom. She stared at each one as if they were about someone she didn't know.

"Isaac never forgave his father for leaving David the land. He threatened more than once to turn us in for selling dope. But he never did. I think he held off partially because of you, not wanting you to get away from him. Or maybe thinking he needed to watch over you.

"He loved you in his crazy way. He couldn't believe how unafraid you were. He never thought for a minute that the way we lived might have something to do with your bravery. Not for a minute. It hurt David so, knowing that Isaac gave him no credit for your fearlessness."

"Did Grandpa bother you the same way he did Dad?" I asked Mom.

She shook her head.

"I got along with Isaac. But I was always part of the problem. 'Berkeley Bolshies' is what your Grandma Alice said he called us. Those photos were the proof he was after."

Mom stopped, reached for one photo, stared at it for a minute, then turned it face down on the table.

"It destroyed Tommy, having to leave. I tried to find him a few times and failed. Once Jane's detective couldn't get a lead, I thought he was dead. Until now."

6

Angie took a bath while I worried my way into the shorts and t-shirt I usually wore to bed. She was smiling when she opened the bathroom door. Her hair was wrapped in a towel, and another was bound around her body, chest to thighs. She grabbed a nightshirt from her suitcase. While we lay side by side, she moved one hand slowly over my back, and then kissed me, her tongue moving around my lips while her hand slid down the length of my thigh.

"You've had a busy week in Lake Woebegone, haven't you?" she said more than asked.

I started to answer, then turned my head away when I started to cry.

Angie reached around me and hugged me to her.

"Poor baby."

I stifled the tears, turned and kissed her. She responded briefly, then sat back. I don't know what she saw in my face but it scared her.

It was a long confession. I told her about the town, the house, and the funeral. Next came Penny. I told her I couldn't forgive myself let alone ask her to forgive me but prayed she would. I went back to the months and months when she and I skated around each other: how that mounted up; how it wasn't an excuse but it had to stop.

She listened and didn't ask questions, though when I got to Penny she stood up and turned to me with a question on her face—*Are you done? How long do I have to endure this? I can't believe what I'm hearing*—something like that. When I quit talking she looked down at her hands. Her shoulders were shaking.

"I was thinking on the way here that it was twelve years. Next month. We met twelve years ago."

I'd been thinking about that too.

"Twelve years. It takes me twelve years to get to Temper and it's your mother who asks me to come. Instead you invite someone you met an hour ago. Do you know what you've done?"

Angie walked across the room to the closet, pulled on jeans and a t-shirt and without a glance back at me headed out of the room and down the stairs. She opened some cupboard doors. I imagined her pouring herself a drink. Instead I heard her bang two skillets together, then down on the wood table, then together again. After that I heard something break and ran down the stairs. Mom was standing in her bedroom door as I passed. Angie was hauling away with a cast iron pan in each hand at the kitchen counter, then smashing the broken pieces into the wooden floor. She looked up when she heard me.

"Tell your father I'll pay for it."

Then she dropped the skillets and headed outside.

Mom looked at me for a moment, went back into her room and closed the door.

I found Angie sitting on the picnic table by the creek.

"What the fuck? You want me to tell you it's OK? Or find someone to sleep with so I can even the score?"

I didn't have an answer.

"Fuck! Fuck, fuck, fuck!"

I kept quiet, looking longingly at her, just that shade taller than me. Her face had gone slack.

"Can we talk?" I asked, begged. "Please?"

She looked at me like I was a stranger.

"What about? New positions or some toy she likes?"

I tried to answer but she cut me off.

"Nothing from you. Nothing! Not a word. You've said enough already."

She came around the table.

"Give me your keys."

"They're in our room. In my jeans."

She nodded.

"I'm going home. My home, since you own this one now."

I watched her go. I was still at the picnic table when I saw the car lights come on. I imagined her in the driver's seat, hypnotized by the road, her hands gripping the steering wheel with a ferocity she would have loved to turn on me.

7

I found Mom in the kitchen drinking a glass of water. She had swept up what she could of the broken tiles. I went to the liquor cabinet and saw we were out of bourbon. Mom went to her room, came back with her travel flask and offered it to me. Scotch. Better than nothing.

"Do you want to tell me what's up?"

I didn't but I didn't want to be alone either.

"Since I've been in Temper I've been sleeping with a woman I met the day after I heard about Grandpa. She followed me here and we spent three days together. I told Angie tonight. You saw the rest."

Mom nodded, poured some scotch into the water in her glass and sipped.

"Did your father meet her?"

"No."

"But you talked to him about her?"

"A little. You know Dad. He doesn't criticize."

"Not like your judgmental mother. I've never been sure whether he's more accepting than me or couldn't care less."

She paused, sipped again.

"What did you want from this current squeeze of yours? Do you know?"

"Not current. Deceased."

"Answer the question."

I paused, trying to get clear with myself.

"I couldn't stop crying when I heard about Grandpa. And I hate Grandpa."

"You don't hate him. You hate what he did. So do I. He was more of a bastard than any of us could imagine, maybe even your father. But you loved him for a time. He was good to you, at least as long as he thought he was your one and only."

"Have it your way. I used to love him. By the time he died I hated him. And I couldn't stop crying once I knew he was dead."

"Grief is grief. You mourn who you mourn."

"The tears weren't about Grandpa. At least not just about him. Penny, the woman I was here with, she told me that. But I wouldn't admit it, that Grandpa was just the trigger."

"You were crying for yourself? Temper?"

"Kind of, yes. For what Temper is to me. I don't get it, any of it—who I am, what it means."

" 'It?' 'Means?' 'Means' like why are you on this earth or why did you screw around behind Angie's back? 'It' like life or sex? You're getting wooey on me."

"I'm a Temper, from Temper, when it was this, . . . this . . . ."

"Place where there was gold."

"Right. And where we came to live, when I was sur-rounded by woods, scorpions, snakes, turtles."

"I've never understood your thing with Temper," Mom said. "You keep harping on it like Temper was your blood type. Why do you keep clinging to your warped memories? I mean really, Joy, you only lived here five years!"

"Exactly! But they count for so much. There's some-thing in this town that eludes me."

"Are we talking treasure chests? Ghosts like that skull you used to talk to all the time?"

"Dad told me about that! You never said a word!"

"What was there to tell? That you talked to bones? That you made up this guy you called Solomon and used him like other girls used their locked journals? It was cute."

"It was OK to talk to a skull then but not think about ghosts now?"

"OK? You live in San Francisco! You could probably open a business with your skull and offer séances."

Mom got up and poured herself more water. I talked to her back.

"There's got to be something about coming from Temper," I went on. "The panning. The quartz. The way you and Dad built our house."

Mom turned and started back to the table.

"You just said what it is. Quartz, the house, your scorpions. It's the people we lived with and loved, and Dad's family who lived here before us, whether we knew them or not. Isn't that enough?"

"No."

"No? Why no?"

I stopped to think.

"There's an undercurrent to everything I once thought I knew about Temper—the Polaroids, the shame thinking about what those photos did to Uncle Thomas; the emptiness I feel looking back at myself as a child living in that orgy of yours."

"It wasn't much of an orgy," Mom said. "We all had jobs and had to get up mornings to get to them. But you think we done you wrong, the way we lived and what we made you put up with? You think you would have been happier if you'd grown up behind a white picket fence eating Wheaties?"

"No."

"Are you sure?"

I hesitated. Mom smiled.

"Sometimes, yeah," I admitted. "Sometimes I wish I were more . . . normal, or less . . . who I am. But you're not being fair. You and Dad, you . . ."

"We what?"

"You let me live in the woods, you let me know things I didn't need or want to know as a kid. You let me get drunk, stoned, high—something—when I didn't know I was and didn't know not to. You . . . weren't there when you were there. You didn't clean my underwear!"

Mom stiffened, then laughed. I laughed too. Then I pushed on.

"You weren't there for me, Mom. Dad wasn't. I know I wasn't molested, I know that Grandpa was wrong—I wasn't in the kind of danger he thought I was. But maybe Cheryl did save me, like she said."

"You can't be serious!"

"Not quite. Almost. Maybe."

She took that in before she started again.

"Some of it was not so bad, is all I want to say. Maybe good for you, maybe not, maybe in-between. It's not fair when children have to teach parents how to do their job. But at least we tried to learn."

I didn't say anything.

"I hope you find what it is you think you're after, the whatever that will make things right for you or let you forgive yourself for what happened to your father and me—and you. My guess is you won't find what you want here or anywhere else. I think life's simpler—simpler than we thought then, simpler than you're making it."

Mom got up from her chair, walked over to me and gently pulled my head to her, where it rested just below her breast. I let it lie there, feeling how fast her heart was pumping.

"I get that you're lost," she said after a moment. "I get that you're miserable. I get that Isaac's death hit you harder than you expected. I know I'm supposed to think that digging into the past and getting the details clear is going to help make things better. But I'm not sure."

Mom paused.

"You had some aura about you when you were a kid. We all felt it. I don't know if it was Temper doing it or your DNA or your scorpions. And I don't know if you lost that because I took you away with me, your dad and I divorced, you studied Psychology or because we just do that—lose a bit of ourselves along the line. When I said I think things are simpler than we made them out to be, I meant it. There are just a few things you do or don't do to yourself and the people you care about. That's all I know."

"Like?"

"You don't go back on people, especially the ones you love. And you don't pretend you don't love them, even when you want to."

She looked around the kitchen for an instant, opened a cupboard, saw a bottle of wine and found a corkscrew.

"You gave up on you and Angie without letting her in on your misery or whatever you want to call it. Hiding unhappiness from someone is as bad as any other secret. Deceit is expensive."

By now she had the wine bottle braced between her legs, ready to pull out the cork.

"I don't know shit, Joy. That should have been apparent to you long before tonight. I'm an aging hippie matron, the kind of old lady kids pass on the street and don't look at twice. I did some adventuring once. It cost me a lot. It seems like it's cost you—who I love more than the sky—even more. Now I get my kicks from crocheting, TV, good food, drinking sometimes, and telling lost tourists how to get back to their tents. I'm not kidding when I say I don't know and I don't care that I don't. If you press me, I think we don't get to. You don't. Angie doesn't. It doesn't matter that we don't."

I must have looked forlorn.

"It's late. Or early. I need sleep. I want to find Tommy. That's important to me. I'll see you when I get up."

She finished pulling out the cork, poured herself a glass, gave me a kiss on the forehead and started toward her room. My room. She went inside but came out a minute later holding something suspended by two fingers like she was carrying a soiled diaper.

"I think this is yours? Or your girlfriend's? It doesn't seem your style. It certainly isn't mine."

It was the "Prospectin'" tee. I took it from Mom.

"I'd get this out of the house before Angie comes back."

"If she does."

"Even if she doesn't."

I nodded. Mom reversed herself and closed the bedroom door behind her.

8

I knew I couldn't sleep. I knocked on Mom's door, went in when she didn't answer and rummaged in her pockets.

"Want something?" Her head was turned away from me.

"Your car keys."

"They're in the car the way I always leave them."

I headed to Main Street. The town clock told me it was five a.m. I was alone, taking in the window displays in a silence that reminded me of when I lived here. The dark glass provided me with shadowy versions of myself. I wondered just how ghostly I could get before the morning light erased me altogether.

I went back to the car, took the "Prospectin'" shirt from the front seat where I'd left it, and walked up to the porch at Temple General. I spread the shirt over the historical plaque that told a visitor that once a long time ago a man named Solomon set down roots here. Then I drove back home.

I made myself coffee and called Angie. Then I called her again. And again. I texted, then called again, begging her to pick up. I warned her that I would call every half hour until she did. I figured that even if she didn't answer, the calls would give me a way to bang my head against the silence and hold myself accountable.

Mom emerged about eight, anxious to be on her way. She downed her coffee and packed herself a lunch. As she was leaving, she asked:

"Have you heard from Angie?"

I shook my head.

"She'll call. She loves you too much not to."

"I thought you didn't know anything about love."

"I don't. I know about Angie."

She headed to her car, then came back.

"I was thinking last night. The stuff about you and scorpions."

"What about them?"

"You never figured that out?"

"What?"

"We taught you how to hold them. No one just does that. Your father learned from his friends. After I got stung

David taught me and we made sure to teach you. You had to know stuff like that, how to deal with scorpions and rattlers, catch fish, build a house. Like Solomon had to know about gold panning, even if he didn't do much of it."

"I wasn't immune from the womb?"

"That was my way to make you special."

"But I wasn't special."

"Not that way."

"How?"

"You were our Joy."

"Not today, Mom."

"Really. We named you that to say how happy we were. Being together and giving birth to you."

Mom was quiet for a moment.

"You were an omen."

"But not the Scorpion Queen."

"Oh yes you were. To Isaac especially. You did get stung. Just once. So we showed you and you tried it while we watched. You dropped the first one, maybe the second. Then you were playing with them."

"But I'm no Tinker Bell."

"Is that so bad?"

"It's not the best time for me to lose my magic."

Mom was quiet for a moment.

"Maybe it's good to realize you learn how to do things rather than are born knowing."

With that, Mom walked out, leaving me to catch up to her logic.

The house was quiet even if I wasn't.

Dad called. I filled him in and he apologized for leaving me in the lurch.

"I was sure you'd figure it out," he told me.

I waited, hoping he'd say more, but he didn't. So I started.

"Why was it Mom's job to tell me about our life here and not yours?"

There was a long pause that made me wonder if Dad heard me.

"No reason. I don't have a good excuse. I try to make things easy on myself when I can and usually that makes it harder."

Which led me to what I really wanted to ask: "What would the Sheriff find if he searched your truck, Dad?"

"What do you think you know?" he flashed back.

"That you went up to the mine the night Grandpa died. That Uncle Thomas was there. And I think Grandpa was there too."

"Next you'll accuse me of killing Dad."

"No. But something happened. Will you tell me?"

"Dad was already dead."

I thought about that.

"Uncle Thomas."

"I'm not sure. I was just wandering that night. I'd had drinks at the Nugget and heard the rumors about Dad wanting to start up the China Mine. So I thought I'd take a look. I got there and saw Tommy walking down the hill carrying Dad. He tried to say something, but he didn't get much out. Then he put Dad down on the ground, looked at me for a moment, turned and walked away."

"You didn't try to grab him? Yell? Stop him?"

"There's a certain way that Tommy has of walking that tells you he's alone and wants to stay that way. And besides, Grandpa was lying there."

"You took Grandpa back to his cabin."

"I figured if someone found Dad in bed people would think he just gave out. And most did. Tommy has had enough trouble in his life. I went back and looked for him the next day but I didn't find anything except the ashes you found."

We were both quiet.

"I'll tell the Sheriff if I need to," he said.

We settled into an uneasy silence.

"I'm sorry about keeping things from you," Dad said. "And I'm sorry about Angie. You'll work it out."

"Sure."

9

In the midst of my misery I remembered the lady in white. I got up, rummaged through my pockets and found her card. She lived in Sonora. I didn't have a car.

I called Preacher. He laughed and said he'd come right over and I could drive him back to the church. As we drove, I asked him,

"Did you ever hear of a woman named Lucy Jin?"

"There was a Jin family who lived in Chinatown. I don't remember them having a daughter that I know of. Why?"

"I'm going to Sonora to see her."

"Why, if you don't mind my asking?"

I parked in front of the church, looked over at him, and said,

"I haven't the faintest idea. She said to come talk to her when I needed to. And I need to."

"That's the best answer I could ask for," Preacher said. "Blessings. The brakes pull sometimes."

Lucy smiled when she saw me, and came over a few minutes later with a notebook in her hand.

"It's so new," I said to her, indicating the library with my hand.

"You expected a converted saloon?" she said.

"I guess."

"Try the Twain-Harte branch. It might be more to your liking."

"No, I don't mean . . ."

"I understand. You're disappointed that Sonora has moved into the twenty-first century. We even have computers, though I admit most of them are several years out of date."

I felt embarrassed. Lucy seemed nonplussed.

"I was hoping you'd come. Can you stay for dinner? We can go somewhere quiet."

I nodded my head and said,

"But I don't know why I'm here."

"I think you do," she said, giving me the kind of look that reminded me of a grade school teacher seeing through one of my lame excuses. Mr. Brenner, sixth grade. "Pay attention to business," he said to us, whether we were talking, trying to read a comic or passing notes back and forth. Business. Stop pretending. Pay attention.

"You had an affair with Grandpa," I said.

"We loved each other is how I thought of it."

I felt awful again.

"I'm sorry."

"Don't be or we'll never get anywhere."

She paused, then handed me the notebook she was carrying.

"Why don't you read this while I finish up here. It will save some time."

It was the kind of journal you might find anywhere: spiral binding, heavy cardboard covers, wide lines. Lucy's handwriting was studied: large, even, neat, set at that angle I remember from endless, useless hours of practice in school.

I was born three months before Isaac. My parents worked for his. Since Isaac and I were the only children, we played together. When it was Isaac's time to start school, Mr.

Temper fixed it so I could attend with him, instead of getting lessons in Miss May's house in Chinatown twice a week with the other Chinese children. Isaac stood up for me the one or two times someone tried to tease me about being Chinese, calling me 'Chink' or 'slant-eyes.' The first time he fought for me Isaac got hit in the cheek and his face rubbed in the dirt by a boy bigger and older than him. But next time when someone said something about me, Isaac already had his belt off when he went out into the playground. Before the boy could reach him Isaac swung that belt straight at the boy's face. No one said anything more after that day.

If I did not have to be back right after school to help my mother with chores Isaac and I would stop by Temper General after class. When we got older he took me out to the woods to teach me how to fish. I was soon as good or better than he was. That riled him until I learned how to make sure he came home with one or two more fish than me. I didn't care. I was there to be with him, and to put my feet in the water to cool myself. Forest air is different from town air. I have always felt that.

---

*We did not tell anyone when we started to make love. I was
afraid for my mother and father if Mr. and Mrs. Temper
knew. I now think Isaac was ashamed of me from the very
beginning. I could not imagine that was so then. I just
thought he was waiting until we were older to let people
know and I trusted him to do that when he was ready.*

*It was a shock when I started hearing Mrs. Temper talk
about Alice Simmons. They were from Sonora and did not
come to Temper often. I had helped my mother serve
dinner for them once and saw Alice sitting at the table,
quiet and polite, not saying anything while the two men
talked at one end and the two women at the other. Isaac
sat across from her looking bored and smiled to me once
when I brought in some dishes.*

*Then I missed a period and started feeling sick morn-
ings. I don't know if Isaac noticed something or because of
Alice, but he started avoiding me so I never could find him
alone to tell him.*

*Finally I told my mother, and she told my father. My
father took me to see Mr. Temper. When he called Isaac*

into the room Isaac denied ever having anything to do with me. Mr. Temper pressed him until Isaac said yes, he had slept with me but so had four or five of his friends. I got up from my chair then, went over to him and dared him to say that to my face. "Slut," he said, and I reached out and ran my fingernails down his cheeks, leaving lines that started to bleed. He screamed and ran from the room. My father started yelling at me in Say Yup, the Cantonese dialect he never spoke in public. Mr. Temper went to see about his son but he was soon back. He apologized to my father and said to me that he believed me. He asked us to give him a few days.

After a week, Mr. Temper called us back to his home. I think he was ashamed, saying things to us he didn't want to say. He told us that Isaac had friends who would swear they had been with me. Whether he believed them or not, he said, enough people would that I'd never be able to live down the shame in Temper. He urged me to leave town and have the baby. He would support me and help me find an adoption agency. I shook my head no. "What do you want, child?" Mr. Temper asked. I surprised him, and my *father, when I said I wanted to keep the baby. It was not what happened in those days. The idea upset everyone. My father started arguing with me. Mr. Temper asked me if I were sure. When I said yes he asked my father to leave the two of us to talk.*

What he had to say did not surprise me. Isaac was engaged to Alice Simmons and insisted that he would marry her. Mr. Temper said he would help me finish high school. If I wanted to go to college he would pay for that. He would provide me with a small amount of money each month to provide for me and my child. He urged me to move to a different town, even different state, to begin my new life. I stood up, thanked him, shook his hand, and left.

That is when I came here, to Sonora. No one knew me and I lived quietly. I had my baby a week early but he was healthy. I named him David, the boy with the slingshot. I thought he would need to know how to defeat his enemies with a rock his only weapon.

That turned out not to be true. A year and a half after David was born Alice Simmons, now Alice Temper, knocked on my door. I had not seen her since the night I served her and her parents dinner though her marriage to Isaac was in all the papers. She was just as lovely as ever. She came, she said, to ask if she and Isaac could adopt David. She knew about Isaac and me. She and Isaac had tried to have a child since their marriage night. She told me that she suffered severe pain each time they were together. Isaac's desperation made him more and more impatient with her. A doctor told her that the pain might be a sign of infertility. They mentioned possible causes, none of which promised an easy remedy. In desperation, a month ago she asked Isaac how he would feel about adoption. He blew up, slapped her, said she was a hopeless imposter of a woman and stalked off to drink. But two days later he agreed. He did not want to know anything about where the child came from as long as it was a boy.

I said yes. I thought I could trust Alice to protect David and Isaac to spoil him. Through Amos and Alice I learned over the years that I was wrong on both counts. But I was not wrong to make him a Temper. He has had a different life from the one he could have had with me. And he has been able, it seems, to raise a beautiful daughter.

I sat quietly for a time waiting for Lucy to close the windows, return some books to their shelves, dim the lights and lock the door. We didn't talk as she led me down the street to a small diner. Finally I said,

"You are Dad's mother."

"One of them. Alice is and always will be."

"You wrote this after you met me?"

She nodded.

"I wanted you to know."

"It must have been so hard for you, giving up your baby."

"Yes. And no. I cried for weeks after I did it. The rooms I rented then felt so empty. I had no one to worry about— worry seems such a sure way to know what matters, don't you think?"

She stared off above my head.

"Alice wrote me and sent me photographs. It's not the same, of course, as raising your own. The world has changed so much since 1948 when your father was born. Then it felt like something Alice had a right to ask and I didn't have a right to say no."

"And you never thought of reaching out to Dad?" I asked.

"I did think about it. Twice. Once when your father and mother came to live here. But Isaac was still alive and things were so bad between him and your father."

"And the second time?"

"That was after Alice died. But I decided that if she had not told him I would respect her silence."

"Do you want to meet him? My dad?"

"I think I am, through you. If you tell him and he wants to meet me, I am happy to. I saw him at the funeral and at the reception. I liked the way he stood. He has a warm face. You can think about what to say or not to say to your father for me."

"That's too much responsibility."

"No. I think you are ready to take responsibility by the shoulders and give it a firm shake."

That made me look down at my soup, then start to cry. Lucy waited and didn't press.

I laid out my story, the recent part—Angie and Penny, Grandpa's funeral, what I'd been learning.

"I'm not sure what to do next," I ended.

"Best to wait, until you know. Know for sure."

"Know what for sure?"

"What you want to do. Not what you want to happen or come out of what you do. Just what you want to do."

I didn't say anything. Finally I asked,

"Are you happy in your life?"

"Very. I am a librarian. I've been other things—a maid, a cook, a secretary, a phone prostitute (there's a demand for Asian voices whatever your looks), and a bus driver for the school district. I have not always been alone as I am now but I have never had anyone who I felt quite as close to as I did Isaac, however deluded I was about him. I tried to retire but I missed the work and the library needed my expertise. I'm regarded as an authority on Gold Country history."

The last came out with more pride than I'd heard from her.

"Have you researched the Tempers?" I asked.

"Of course!"

None of what Lucy told me was good news. It turns out

Solomon had a competitor, a Mr. Brian Klegg, who opened a general store and undersold Solomon. Mr. Klegg was not against selling to the Chinese miners or the Mexicans who lived nearby.

"Solomon Temper was not a friend of the Chinese," Lucy explained. "They owned and worked some good mines in the area. When he made offers to buy them out, like he did other miners, they said no to him. They were not in debt to him, like a lot of the white miners, and could get the credit they needed from Klegg.

"From here we move into conjecture. What is a fact is that one night there was a raid on Chinatown. Men wearing bags and cloths over their faces rode in on horseback, tore down the tents and set fire to them, scattering the Chinese and killing six. No one ever proved who the men were. But the story goes that Klegg came to the camp the next day and noticed among the horse prints one horse that was absent a shoe. He tracked the horse to Solomon's stable behind his store. Of course that did not prove anything, but Klegg went around town telling everyone that Solomon was the ringleader.

"A few days later, Klegg disappeared. Two days after that, his body was found near one of the mines. A jury called it suicide, but a reporter from the Sacramento newspaper wrote that a doctor in town told him Klegg had died from a bullet in his back. That's not generally the way of a suicide."

"Did they find a shoeless horse print?"

She laughed.

"I've no idea. But it does not pay to criticize a Temper, I think that's the moral of the story."

Lucy did admire Amos, who stood by his word.

I had one more question.

"My uncles—if Alice couldn't have children . . ."

Lucy smiled.

"Alice didn't confide in me, except that one time. So I don't know the details. I do know Alice traveled to San Francisco to see specialists. In those days if there was a problem about having children doctors liked to blame the woman. Let's just say the doctors were wrong or they were able to help Alice in time."

Lucy smiled, more to herself than me.

"Maybe I was the anomaly when it came to Isaac's ability to bear children. If I were to guess, which I won't to anyone but you, I am pretty sure your uncles don't have the same father as our David. I think he was someone Alice knew in the years she lived in Sonora, before her marriage. I remember a period when she visited her parents more regularly than usual. That's all I will say."

When we finished our meal, I gave Lucy a hug, took her notebook with me and promised I would see her again before I left Temper.

"Maybe you'll never leave," she said. "Then we can have dinners like this every week."

10

Mom was already home when I got back.

"I thought I heard something," she said. "Some rustling in the bush. But every time I walked that way it stopped."

She asked where I had been. I wasn't ready to talk about Lucy.

"With Preacher," I said.

She nodded like she wasn't listening, squeezed my hand and headed for bed. I walked down to the creek. Sometime that night I must have walked back to the house, climbed the stairs and fallen asleep. I woke up with light coming in from the deck windows. Mom headed back up to the mine. I stayed home and called Angie every half-hour. I read and reread Lucy's account. I could only guess that Grandpa never knew David was his own son, and never forgave him for not being. And what did I do with the fact—if it was a fact—that Aaron and Saul didn't come from Temper blood as Isaac thought they did?

234

Lucy was right: it didn't pay to cross a Temper. It didn't pay to be one either. Or not be one. Or think you were one when you weren't.

What other secrets were buried in the family graves?

It was about four in the afternoon. Mom still wasn't home. I was sitting on the front deck, staring out at the gravel driveway. I looked up to find Uncle Thomas standing in the house doorway. He looked thinner than when I saw him four days ago. He wore the same long-sleeved flannel shirt—the tails tucked into his jeans now, with a rope through the belt loop. He had the necklace with the rail spike dangling from his right hand.

"Hello niece."

"I'm glad to see you, Uncle Thomas."

"It's your birthday, Miss Why. I've lost count of mine. I wish you the same."

I had forgotten. Again.

"It was day before yesterday."

"Close."

"How long have you been living there, by the mine?" I asked him.

He paused, counted on his fingers.

"Four months. Maybe. I came after the rains."

April.

"Now Mom and I can help," I said.

"Help. I've always wondered about that."

"Wondered what?"

"About help. About people who try to help."

He stared at me.

"Are you here digging for gold?"

"No. It's a long story."

"I love to listen," he said. "I hear the birds, the cars, the wind. I hear wood burning. It keeps me quiet, listening. Long story, short, no matter. Tell me. It will be good to listen."

The last weeks tumbled out, from Grandpa's funeral to Penny to my discoveries about Mom, Dad, and Grandpa. Just how many confessions would I make before I had another story to tell?

He stood still while I talked. He smiled when I stopped.

"I don't miss the soaps when I can listen to you."

"I'm not sure that's a compliment, Uncle," I said. "I feel like a cliché."

"We all are, Missy. It is only a matter which."

He stared down at the wood on the deck, then back up at me.

"And David? Is he here?"

I shook my head, then added what Dad had told me about the night he saw Grandpa in Uncle Thomas' arms.

He nodded.

"I'm sorry he found me, your grandpa. I was so careful."

He paused.

"What happened?" I asked.

"I was asleep in the mine. Then he was banging on my head with his fists, sitting on me. I rolled around so he fell off."

"Did you know it was Grandpa?"

"It couldn't be no one else."

He stopped talking, moved a few steps forward, and sat down at the picnic table across from me.

"I tried to stand up. He started running at me. I turned and he jumped on my back. No telling what you can do when you're angry. And he was calling me things, yelling. Not true what he said."

He stopped, smiled at me.

"I would never hurt you. He should know that. Never ever."

"I know, Uncle."

He nodded.

"I twisted, trying to get him off, then went over. On top of him. His hands let go. I stood up. He kicked out once, twice, and stared at me. His arm jumped and fell. There was no more to him. His eyes opened and little bubbles came out of his mouth. I knew."

"You knew he was dead?"

"You know. It's not the first time. You see it, moving around like I do."

"And then?"

"I picked him up. To take him home."

"And you saw Dad."

"I didn't say hello."

"You turned away," I said.

"I don't know why."

He nodded his head again.

"Wish he let me alone. You, your mom, your dad. I wish that man let us be."

I waited but he didn't say anything else about that night. When he turned his head and looked at me again, he had come back to today.

"I've missed your mom. I'm thinking about her lately. You. This house. My best home ever."

"I'm sorry you had to leave, Uncle Thomas. It was my fault."

He lifted his hand towards me and then threw it back behind him.

"You meant no harm. No harm no fault. You showed him what you saw. He saw different. You couldn't know."

"Is this your first time back?"

"No no. I come and go. I stay in the mine, with the ghosts. Good neighbor, a ghost. You remember the ones I told you about?"

I nodded.

"You ever seen a ghost?" he asked.

"I used to talk to a skull."

"Ghosts are not there for you and me. They got their own woes. Like my friends at the mine. They go their own way and let me be."

He was quiet, staring down at the tabletop.

"It isn't worth the fuss, love, seems to me. Send it downstream is better. I love you and your ma. I keep you all with me and send the hurt downstream."

"So you aren't afraid anymore?"

"You can't not be afraid. Why else come home? Are you home, here?"

"Maybe. There's trouble all around me. That makes it home, right?"

"That's good. Trouble, home. I didn't know till you said it why I came."

I laughed.

"You don't sound afraid," Uncle Thomas said. "You're the same Miss Why. Scorpion Queen."

I remembered the dog tag, reached into a pocket and handed it to him.

"I found this under a bush, where you were."

He smiled and rubbed his thumb across it.

"I wondered where it went. Glad it came to you."

He put it on the tabletop, made a pillow of his hands over it and put his head down.

"I love you all."

"I love you too, Uncle."

"Keep warm, niece."

It wasn't a moment later that I heard a faint snore. I went into the house, got the blanket from Mom's bed and slid it over Uncle Thomas' shoulders. Then I went back inside to get my phone and let Mom know. When I came out he was gone. No Uncle Thomas, blanket, or dog tag. I rushed through the house and property but he had disappeared as quietly as he had the night I saw him at the China Mine.

I called Mom but got no answer. She turned into the driveway fifteen minutes later. When I told her what had happened she was frantic, ran circles around me and the house. She insisted I repeat the story, then rushed off again in her car. She didn't return until dark, forlorn. The duffle bag was gone. She found the dog tag dangling from a rusty nail along one of the beams.

11

Mom and I passed the next day walking back and forth through the house, rubbing shoulders, unable to say anything to each other. Mom went out to the mine to look once more, came home, then drove into town and came back with some whiskey. The bottle sat unopened on the kitchen table. Exhaustion caught up with me about eight at night and I disappeared into sleep.

I slept until five the next morning, jumped out of bed, grabbed a towel, and drove up to the quarry. I watched as the morning made its way across the sky, Penny's necklace in my hand. I walked down to the water and slipped in. I drifted, stretching my arms and legs out into a starfish, and let go of the necklace. It floated for a moment before it disappeared.

When I turned into the gate I saw my Prius—Angie's Prius—parked near the house. I ran up the stairs. Angie and

Mom were sitting at the kitchen table. Mom was crying. Angie was holding one of her hands. They glanced my way when I came in, Mom lost in her tears, Angie's face tense.

"Act surprised," Mom said.

"I don't need to act this time," I said. I walked over to Angie, knelt beside her chair and buried my face in her lap. She let go of Mom's hand and combed her fingers through my hair.

"You're supposed to be in Houston or Vegas or somewhere."

"I think I'm supposed to be here. It's your birthday. Or was a day or two or three ago."

I reached up and kissed her.

"Can you stay?" Meaning, do you want to?

"Not long."

Mom sat watching us, then picked up the still-unopened bottle of whiskey.

"Seems like a good morning for a drink or two, daughter. Then bed. Whatever you two do to each other, do it quietly."

I stood up and hugged her. She hugged me for a second,

bent down to kiss Angie on the cheek, thanked her and went to her room.

"Your Mom is so sad. She said that you were a mess. You don't look a mess—not to me anyway. Not the way I feel a mess."

"I'm messier than you."

"Bet not."

"I'm so glad you're here," I said to her.

"I'm glad I'm here too. I've missed you. And I'm mad at myself for missing you."

"Let's go upstairs."

She stood up, pulled away when I tried to kiss her.

"I'm not here for long."

"I heard you when you said that."

"Not just because of work. I need time. I'm not through with what you've done to me."

I nodded.

"You're dumb not to know how important you are. Very very dumb."

"I'm not always dumb. I fell in love with you."

"Don't go sticky on me."

"Promise," I said. Then I cupped my palm to her cheek.

12

Angie gave us the night. We spent most of it lying next to each other talking. We made love, walked down to the creek, then back to the house. We were about to get into bed again when Angie jumped up, ran down the stairs and out to the car.

She came back holding a small brown paper bag.

"This was supposed to be wrapped. It was supposed to be for your birthday but I never got to give it to you."

Inside was a cobalt blue doorknob.

"This one actually works," she said.

I felt the mechanisms catch as I turned the handles.

"They all do," I told her, and reached over to hug her. She seemed to settle into the hug for a moment, then pulled away.

"I didn't say so before but I'm here because your mom called. This isn't a new start."

"I don't understand."

"Yes you do. You really fucked up, Joy. There's nothing you can say right now to make me forget that or forgive you. I know I love you, but that's not enough to make me trust you."

"What else can I do?"

"I don't know. Figure something out."

"I can't do that alone."

"You're not going to do it with me. I need time away from you. If it feels right, I will stay a day or so longer. But then I'm going back to San Francisco, and from there to Houston and Las Vegas. When I get back I want your stuff out of the apartment."

I started to protest but heard a truck rolling in across the gravel out front. It pulled to a stop, the lights went off, and there were steps on the deck stairs. I threw on my shorts and tee and ran downstairs. Dad was walking through the glass doors.

"What are you doing here?" I asked, running up to give him a hug.

"I thought you might need me," he said, hugging me back.

Mom came out of her room in underpants, tugging a t-shirt over her face. When she saw it was Dad she grabbed the edges of the tee and hurriedly pulled it down over her navel. Angie took that moment to run down the stairs, not fully clothed either. She saw Dad and started to laugh. Dad stood there, embarrassed. He said he'd be off and check in later. We grabbed his arms and pulled him into the kitchen. He saw the broken tiles and walked over to examine them.

"You're not as done here as you thought, Dad," I said.

He nodded, confused.

13

I tried to imagine what it would mean to Lucy, Dad, Mom, and me when Dad met Lucy. If Dad met Lucy. I tried, but couldn't. So I followed Lucy's advice: I wanted Dad to know so I told him. Or let her tell him.

The morning after Dad arrived I asked him to walk down to the creek with me.

"Do you remember the woman in white we saw at Grandpa's burial?"

He nodded.

"She talked to me briefly at the reception and gave me her card. Her name is Lucy Jin. She's a librarian in Sonora."

Dad was staring off at the creek while he listened half-heartedly.

"She told me she once knew Grandpa and invited me to come see her. I went a few days ago. We had a long talk about Grandpa and you."

Dad turned to me then.

"How would she know about me? Or Dad?"

"I was hoping you'd ask."

I handed him Lucy's notebook. And his glasses.

"I'm going to the house to get us some coffee, give you time to read."

I left him with the creek for company. When I came back he looked at me and smiled. I put my coffee down and stood behind him with my hands on his shoulders. He put one of his over mine, only letting go when he needed to turn a page.

After Mom and Angie had their turns with the notebook I invited Lucy to the house. What it came down to was sad but simple: Dad was mistreated, Grandpa was dumb as a deer, Grandma too forgiving for her own good, or Dad's.

I told Preacher, who clapped his hands together.

"This is not the only family in this town where something like this happened," he told me. "There are too many to name, and I can't name them even if I wanted to. I'm just glad the times are changing."

———

14

The morning after everyone left, I drove up to China Mine. I had just bent down to pick up a rusty fork when I heard heavy steps approaching the entrance. It was the Sheriff.

"Looking for something?" he asked.

"Nothing in particular," was all I could get out.

He was quiet, his eyes hidden under his hat brim.

"The way I see it," he said, "someone's been camping around here. There's fresh ash in that clearing, not to mention the whatever-it-is you just slipped into your pocket."

I pulled out the fork and squeezed the handle in my fist.

"No idea who, I suppose?" the Sheriff continued.

"I don't get up here much," I said. "Just thought I'd take a look before my uncles sold off the property."

The Sheriff nodded, then went on.

"I've known your family since I was old enough to pay for candy at Temper General. Your grandpa was an ornery cuss who spat meanness and would have drunk himself to death sooner or later. But he didn't die from bourbon. Someone's not saying something and that riles me."

I refused to let the Sheriff stare me down.

"Dad once said to me that he didn't believe truth would set you free. I argued with him, insisting that lies won't either. Now I think both of us had a point."

The Sheriff took that in, nodded, reached out a hand and we shook.

"You've got more Temper in you than I thought," he said to me. "That's not entirely a compliment." Then he turned and headed for his car.

"And a bit of Lucy Jin," I said to myself as I watched him go.

I stayed in Temper through one of the hottest Augusts on record. I drove to Sonora every Wednesday to have dinner with Lucy. I spent more than one afternoon in the Historical Museum to learn about the local natives, the Maidu, who believed that the souls of the dead revisit old haunts to reclaim their lives. That helped me come to terms with

Uncle Thomas and his ghosts even if it didn't do much for mine. I studied a little geology to understand why there was gold in California in the first place: the old seabed covered with minerals and lava from volcanic explosions, the tectonic eruptions, the nuggets that surfaced in fields of quartz and gravel beds along streams.

I looked up the word "forgive" and found out that it originally had to do with giving up a deed, only later with pardoning a person. Solomon and Constance were driven west by greed; that much was certain. But there are lots of greeds, not all of them sins. Behind their acquisitiveness was a hunger. And when we're hungry, we take more than we need. We overreach, we injure others. If we realize what we've done, we ask forgiveness. If we last long enough, we do it again, and again. Or some of us do, until we realize there's abundance enough, and it's not for lack of satisfaction that we still want.

Once Cheryl closed with my uncles, she let me spend a last afternoon in Temper General. I watched the sun cross the floor planks, polished by decades of boots and moccasins, clogs and lace-ups. This had been my second home. Lucy's too, for a time. I tried to conjure a link with the shoppers but I couldn't join their stories to mine.

I spent hours taking self-portraits: in front of a mirror, with a tripod and timer, in black and white and color. I looked washed out, my cheeks hollow. I tried to decide who I most resembled—Mom, Dad, Lucy, Grandpa, Angie. I shot close-ups of the bruises on my neck from Penny's attack and watched as they disappeared.

What I had done didn't.

I went through Dad's photo collection again and again until I realized I was looking for something no photo can capture, like what they say a bird's song sounds like if you slow it down, imagine what it croons to its mate rather than us tone-deaf humans. I thought a lot about Mom, Dad and the life I lived as the Scorpion Queen. I didn't want to admonish. I couldn't even decide what the crime might have been: was it hiding, or flaunting, adult lives before a minor? I know they wanted to offer me what no one ever gave them: the freedom to grow up surrounded by people who loved each other and loved me. It didn't work out the way they planned but what does? We make do, as they have.

I carried Angie's birthday doorknob with me wherever I went. I wasn't sure if it was my way to comfort or punish myself. I would rub the faceted glass, turn the handles, set it on the kitchen table and stare at it while I ate. The granola that became my breakfast, lunch, and dinner burned across the top of my mouth. It hurt more knowing it was a recipe I got from Angie.

I was choosing some of Dad's photos to bring back to San Francisco when I heard an explosive crack from the direction of the creek. I rushed out to see a huge oak branch lying across the remnants of the picnic table. The branch had split off about four feet from the trunk.

I'd seen this before. Summer limb drop. No one knows why, Dad told me the first time it happened. Something to do with the heat? Moisture buildup? I couldn't remember.

The tabletop had split into a V around the fallen branch. It was beyond repair, I decided. I stared up at the jagged bark that hung about three feet above me on the trunk. The rest of the limb would have to go. Then I'd need to find someone to trim the bark at the break to make sure the tree survived. Cleaning up would give me something to do while I waited for Angie to call. Or stopped waiting.